EX LIBRIS

VINTAGE **CLASSICS**

E. F. BENSON

Edward Frederick Benson was born on 24 July, 1867 in Berkshire, the son of a future Archbishop of Canterbury, and one of six children. He studied at King's College, Cambridge and at the British School of Archaeology in Athens. Benson's first book, *Dodo*, was published to popular acclaim in 1893 and was followed by over a hundred books, including novels, histories, biographies and ghost stories. In 1920 Benson became a full-time tenant of Lamb House in Rye, which had once been home to the novelist Henry James. Rye provided the setting for the well-loved Mapp and Lucia stories and their author served three terms as mayor of Rye in the late 1930s. E. F. Benson died on 29 February, 1940.

ALSO BY E. F. BENSON

Mapp and Lucia

Queen Lucia

Miss Mapp

Lucia in London

Lucia's Progress

Trouble for Lucia

E. F. BENSON

Ghost Stories

SELECTED AND INTRODUCED BY

Mark Gatiss

VINTAGE

1 3 5 7 9 10 8 6 4 2

Vintage
20 Vauxhall Bridge Road,
London SW1V 2SA

Vintage Classics is part of the Penguin Random House group of companies whose addresses can be found at global.penguinrandomhouse.com

These stories have been selected from *The Room in the Tower and Other Stories*, *Spook Stories* and *More Spook Stories*, published in Great Britain in 1912, 1928 and 1934 respectively

First published in Great Britain by Vintage Classics in 2016

www.vintage-books.co.uk

A CIP catalogue record for this book is available from the British Library

ISBN 9781784871901

Typeset in 10.75/13.25 pt Sabon
Jouve (UK), Milton Keynes
Printed and bound by Clays Ltd, St Ives plc

Penguin Random House is committed to a sustainable future for our business, our readers and our planet. This book is made from Forest Stewardship Council® certified paper.

Contents

Introduction

Even in a land of eccentrics, the Benson family were *particular*.

Paterfamilias Edward proposed marriage to Minnie when she was only twelve. He went on to become the Archbishop of Canterbury, she a startlingly visible gay woman who liked to be known as 'Ben' and was referred to by Gladstone as 'the cleverest woman in Europe'.

Edward and Minnie's troubled union bore six children, four of whom survived into somewhat fey adulthood. The fifth, Edward Frederick, went on to become a figure skater, social butterfly and one of the funniest writers these isles ever produced. Though most famous today for his sublime Mapp and Lucia stories, 'Fred' Benson was renowned in his day for his ghostly tales or, as he preferred them, his 'spook stories'.

Benson's acquaintanceship with the supernatural (barring his family's cachet with the heavenly realm) may perhaps be traced to his attendance at the very first of M. R. James's Christmas ghost story readings at King's College, Cambridge. Though he was never close to the Master of the Ghost Story (unlike his brother Arthur), their work may be said to sit companionably together, James's air of dusty academia sprinkled with a concoction all Fred's own.

Benson's ghostly world will be familiar to Mapp and Lucia enthusiasts. It is a place of summer leases and house-envy, of confirmed bachelorhood and of (sometimes literally) monstrous women. But there are surprises here too. The very funny 'Spinach' properly skewers mediumship, yet in other stories, such as the scary 'In the Tube', he seems genuinely fascinated by the notion of 'astral projection'. 'The Man Who Went Too Far' (much admired by H. P. Lovecraft) hints at a fascination with an ancient and dangerous pagan sensibility. The ghastly 'Mrs Amworth', though she sets up 'an example of luncheon parties and little dinners' that could exist in Tilling, proves to have altogether darker appetites.

I love these stories, not only for their grace and easy style, but because they show the incredible range of Benson's taste; by turns sly, hilarious, horrifying and strange. It's easy to imagine Fred in the garden of Lamb House, Rye, smiling to himself in the summer sunshine, his nib scratching away as he took his imagination spiralling down ever murkier avenues. The most famous stories retain a unique power. 'The Room in the Tower' is properly creepy ('*Jack will show you to your room. I have given you the room in the tower*') and 'The Bus-Conductor' has assumed almost the status of an urban legend thanks to its inclusion in the legendary Ealing portmanteau film *Dead of Night*. 'Negotium Perambulans' and 'And No Bird Sings' nod to the slithering monstrosities of M. R. James and the extraordinarily weird and grim 'Caterpillars' is perhaps a ghost story like no other.

If you're new to Benson's 'Spook Stories', then you're in for a treat; if you're returning to them, then this handsome edition will hopefully reacquaint you with the shades of some old friends. In any event, it is wonderful to think that Fred Benson's *particular* approach to the ghost story will always be appreciated by lovers of the genre.

He never married. As the obituaries used to say.

Mark Gatiss, London 2016

Spinach

Ludovic Byron and his sister Sylvia had adopted these pretty, though quite incredible, names because those for which their injudicious parents and godparents were responsible were not so suitable, though quite as incredible. They rightly felt that there was a lack of spiritual suggestiveness in Thomas and Caroline Carrot which would be a decided handicap in their psychical careers, and would cool rather than kindle the faith of those inquirers who were so eager to have séances with the Byrons.

The change, however, had not been made without earnest thought on their parts, for they were two very scrupulous young people, and wondered whether it would be 'acting a lie' thus to profess to be what they were not, and whether, in consequence, the clearness of their psychical sight would be dimmed. But they found to their great joy that their spiritual guides or controls, Asteria and Violetta, communicated quite as freely with the Byrons as with the Carrots, and by now they called each other by their assumed names quite naturally, and had almost themselves forgotten that they had ever been other than what they were styled on their neat professional engagement-cards.

While it would be tedious to trace Ludovic's progress from the time when it was first revealed to him that he had rare mediumistic gifts down to the present day, when he was quite at the head of his interesting profession, it is necessary to explain the manner in which his powers were manifested. When the circle was assembled (fees payable in advance), he composed himself in his chair, and seemed to sink into a sort of trance, in which Asteria took possession of him and communicated through his mouth with the devotees. Asteria, when living on the material plane had been a Greek maiden of ancient Athens, who had become a Christian and suffered martyrdom in Rome about the same time as St Peter. She had wonderful things to tell them all about her experiences on this earth, a little vague, perhaps, as was only natural after so long a lapse of time, but she spoke dreamily yet convincingly about the Parthenon and the Forum and the Aegean sea (so blue), and the catacombs (so black), and the beautiful Italian and Greek sunsets, and this was all the more remarkable because Ludovic had never been outside the country of his birth.

But far more interesting to the circle, any of whom could take a ticket for Rome or Athens and see the sunsets and the catacombs for themselves, were the encouraging things she said about her present existence. Everyone was wonderfully happy and busy helping those who had lately passed over to the other side, and they all lived in an industrious ecstasy of spiritual progress. There were refreshments and relaxations as well, quantities of the most beautiful flowers and exquisite fruits and crystal rivers and azure mountains, and flowing robes and delightful habitations. None of these things was precisely material; you 'thought' a flower or a robe, and there it was!

Asteria knew many of the friends and relatives, who had passed over, of Ludovic's circle, and they sent through her loving messages and sweet thoughts. There was George, for instance – did any of the sitters know George? Very often somebody did know George. George was the late husband of one of the sitters, or the father of another, or the little son, who had passed over, of a third, and so George would say how happy he was, and how much love he sent. Then Asteria would tell them that Jane wanted to talk to her dear one, and if nobody knew Jane, it was Mary. And Asteria explained quite satisfactorily how it was that, among all the thousands who were continually passing over, just those who had friends and relations among the ladies and gentlemen who sat with Ludovic Byron were clever enough to 'spot' Asteria as being his spiritual guide, who would put them into communication with their loved ones. This was due to currents of sympathy which immediately drew them to her.

Then, when the séance had gone on for some time, Asteria would say that the power was getting weak, and she would bid them goodbye and fade into silence. Presently Ludovic came out of his trance, and they would all tell him how wonderful it had been. At other séances he would not go into trance at all, but Asteria used his hand and his pencil, and wrote pages of automatic script in quaint, slightly foreign English, with here and there a word in strange and undecipherable characters, which was probably Greek. George and Jane and Mary were then dictating to Asteria, who caused Ludovic to write down what she said, and sometimes they were very playful, and did not like their wife's hat or their husband's tie, just by way of showing that they were really there.

And then any member of the circle could ask Asteria questions, and she gave them beautiful answers.

Sylvia and her guide, Violetta, were not in so advanced a stage of development as Ludovic and Asteria; indeed, it was only lately that Sylvia had discovered that she had psychical gifts and had got into touch with her guide. Violetta had been a Florentine lady of noble birth, and was born (on the material plane) in the year 1492, which was a very interesting date, as it made her an exact contemporary of Savonarola and Leonardo da Vinci. She had often heard Savonarola preach, and had seen Leonardo at his easel, and it was splendid to know that Savonarola often preached now to enraptured audiences, and that Leonardo was producing pictures vastly superior to anything he had done on earth. They were not material pictures exactly, but thought-pictures. He thought them, and there the pictures were. This corresponded precisely with what Asteria had said about the flowers, and was therefore corroborative evidence.

This winter and spring had been a very busy time for Ludovic, and Mrs Sapson, one of the most regular attendants at his séances, had been trying to persuade him to go for a short holiday. He was very unwilling to do so, for he was giving five full séances every day (which naturally 'mounted up'), and he was loth to abandon, even for a short time, the work that so many people found so enlightening. But then Mrs Sapson had been very clever, and had asked Asteria at one of the séances whether he ought not to take a rest, and Asteria distinctly said: 'Wisdom counsels prudence; be it so.' After the séance was over, therefore, Mrs Sapson, strong in spiritual support, renewed her arguments with redoubled force.

She was a large, emphatic widow, who received no end of messages from her husband William. He had been a choleric stockbroker on this plane, but his character had marvellously mellowed and improved, and now he knew what a waste of time it had been to make so much money and lose so much temper.

'Dear Mr Ludovic,' she said, 'you must have a rest. You can't fly in the face of sweet Asteria. Besides, I have just got a lovely plan for you. I own a charming little cottage near Rye, which is vacant. My tenant has – has suddenly quitted it. It is a dear little place, everything quite ready for you. No expense at all, except what you eat and drink, and seabathing and golf at your door. Such a place for quiet and meditation, and – who knows – some wonderful visitor (not earthly, of course, for there are no bothering neighbours) might come to you there.'

Of course, this charming offer made a great difference. Ludovic felt that he could give up his spiritual work for a fortnight with less of a wrench than was possible when he thought that he would have to pay for lodgings. He expressed his gratitude in suitable terms, and promised to consult Sylvia, who at the moment was engaged with Violetta. She leaped at the idea when it was referred to her, and the matter was instantly settled.

The two were chatting together on the eve of their departure.

'Wonderfully kind of Mrs Sapson,' said Ludovic. 'But it's odd that she didn't offer us the cottage before. She was wanting me to take a holiday a month ago.'

'Perhaps the tenant has only just left,' said Sylvia.

'That may be so. Dear me, the country and seabreezes! How nice. But I don't mean to be idle.'

'Golf?' suggested Sylvia. 'Isn't it very difficult?'

He walked across to the table and took up a square parcel, which had just been delivered.

'No, not golf,' he said. 'But I am going to take up spirit photography. It pays very – I mean it's very helpful. So I've bought a camera and some rolls of films, and the developing and fixing solutions. I shall do it all myself. I used to photograph when I was a boy.'

'That must have cost a good deal of money,' said Sylvia, who had a great gift for economy.

'Ten pounds, but don't look pained; I think it's worth it. Besides, we get our lodging free. And if I have the power of spirit-photography, it will repay us over and over again.'

'Explain the process to me,' said Sylvia.

'Well, it's very mysterious, but there's no doubt that if a medium who has got the gift takes a photograph, there sometimes appears on the negative what is called an "extra". In other words, if I took a photograph of you there might appear on the film not only your photograph, but that of some spirit, connected with you or the place, standing by you, or perhaps its face floating in the air near you. It would make another branch of our work, it would bring in fresh clients. The old ones too; I think they want something new. Mrs Sapson would love a photograph of herself with her William leaning over her shoulder. Anyhow, it's worth trying. I shall practise down at the cottage.'

He put the parcel containing the photographic apparatus with other property for packing, and made himself comfortable in his chair.

'I want you to work too,' he said. 'I want you to develop your *rapport* with Violetta. There's nothing like practice.

Mediumistic power is just as much a gift as music. But you must practise on the piano to be able to play.'

The two were alone, and the utmost confidence existed between them. They talked to each other with a frankness which would have appalled their sitters.

'Sometimes I wonder whether I have any mediumistic power at all,' she said. 'I get in a dreamy sort of state when I am writing automatic script; but is Violetta really communicating, or am I only putting down the thoughts of my subconscious self? Or when Asteria speaks through you is she really an independent intelligence, or is she part of your own?'

Ludovic was in a very candid mood.

'I don't know, and I don't care,' he said. 'But my conscious self certainly can't invent all the things Asteria says, so they come from outside my normal perceptions. And then, after all, Asteria tells things about George and Jane, and so on, concerning their life on earth, which I never knew at all.'

'But their relations who are sitting with you know them,' said Sylvia. 'Isn't it possible that you may get at those facts through telepathy?'

'Yes, but then that's extremely clever of me if I do,' said Ludovic. 'And it's just as reasonable to say that it's Asteria. Besides, if it's all me, how do you account for it that Asteria sometimes says something which goes against all my intentions and inclinations? For instance, when she said, "Wisdom counsels prudence: be it so", in answer to Mrs Sapson's asking if I was not overworked and wanted a holiday, that quite contradicted my own wishes. I didn't want to go for a holiday at all. Therefore it looks as if Asteria was an external intelligence controlling me.'

'Subconsciously you might have known you wanted a holiday,' said the ingenious Sylvia.

'That's far-fetched. Better stick to Asteria. Besides, I sincerely believe that sometimes things come to me from outside my consciousness. And I don't know – not always, that's to say – what Asteria has been telling them while I'm in trance. Sometimes it really astonishes me.'

He poured out a moderate whisky-and-soda.

'I'm looking forward to a holiday from séances,' he said, 'now that it's settled, for, frankly, Asteria has been a little thin and feeble lately. And I'm not sure that Mrs Sapson doesn't think so too. I think she feels that she's heard about all that Asteria has got to say, and it would never do to lose her as a sitter. That's why I should very much like to find that I can produce spirit photographs. It – it would vary the menu.'

They took with them a grim and capable general servant called Gramsby, and arrived next afternoon at Mrs Sapson's cottage. It was romantically situated near a range of great sand-dunes which ran along the coast, and was only a few minutes' walk from the sea. The place was very remote; a minute village with a shop or two and a cluster of fishermen's huts stood half a mile away, and inland there stretched the empty levels of the Romney marsh away to Rye, which smouldered distantly in the afternoon sunlight. The cottage itself was an enchanting abode, built of timber and rough-cast, with a broad verandah facing south, and a gay little garden in front. Inside, on the ground floor, there were kitchen and dining-room, and a large living-room with access to the verandah. This was well and plainly furnished and had an open fireplace with a wide hearth for a wood fire and an immense chimney. Logs were ready laid there and, indeed, the whole house had the aspect of having been lately tenanted. Upstairs there were sunny bedrooms facing south, which, overlooking the sand-dunes, gave a restful view of the sea beyond; it was impossible to conceive a more tranquil haven for an overworked medium.

They had a hasty cup of tea, and hurried out to enjoy the last hours of daylight in exploration among the sand-dunes and along the beach, and came back soon after sunset. Though the day had been warm, the evening air had a nip in it, and Sylvia gave a little shiver as they stepped in from the verandah to the sitting-room.

'It's rather cold,' she said. 'I think I'll light the fire.'

Ludovic shared her sensations.

'An excellent idea,' he said. 'And we'll draw the curtains and be cosy. What a charming room! I shall take some interiors tomorrow – time exposure, I think they told me, for an interior.'

Their supper was soon ready, and presently they came back to the sitting-room and laid out a hectic Patience. But they were both strangely absent-minded, neglecting the most glaring opportunities for getting spaces and putting up kings.

'I can't concentrate on it tonight,' said Ludovic. 'I feel as if someone was trying to attract my attention . . . I wonder if Asteria wants to communicate.'

Sylvia looked up at him.

'Now it's very odd that you should say that,' she observed. 'I feel exactly as if Violetta was wanting to come through, and yet it doesn't seem quite like Violetta.'

He gave an uneasy glance round the room.

'A curious sensation,' he said. 'I have the consciousness of some presence here which isn't quite Asteria. But it may be she. Tiresome of her, if it is, for she ought to know I came down here for a holiday, considering that she recommended it herself. I think I'll get a pencil and paper, and see if she wants to say anything.'

He composed himself in a chair, with the stationery for Asteria on his knee.

'Ask her a question or two, Sylvia,' he said, 'when I go off.'

Sylvia waited till her brother's eyelids fluttered and fell.

'Is that you, Asteria?' she asked.

His hand twitched and quivered. Then the pencil scribbled 'Certainly not' in large, firm letters, quite unlike Asteria's pretty writing.

Sylvia asked if it was Violetta, but got an emphatic denial.

'Who is it, then?' she said.

And then a very absurd thing happened. The pencil spelt out 'Thomas Spinach'.

Sylvia was puzzled for a moment. Then the explanation occurred to her, and she laughed.

'Wake up, dear,' she said to Ludovic. 'It says it is Thomas Spinach. Of course, that's your subconscious self trying to remember Carrot.'

But Ludovic did not stir, and to her surprise the pencil began writing again.

'I don't know who you are,' wrote the unknown control. 'But I'm Spinach, young Spinach. And – ' there was a long pause – 'I want you to help me. I can't remember . . . I'm very unhappy.'

As she followed the words, there suddenly came a very loud rap on the wall just above her, which considerably startled her, for why, if 'Spinach' was an attempt on the part of Ludovic's subconsciousness to write 'Carrot', should he announce his presence? She sprang up, and shook Ludovic by the shoulder.

'Wake up,' she said. 'There's a strange spirit here, and I don't like it. Wake up, Ludovic.'

He came drowsily to himself.

'Hullo!' he said. 'Anything been happening? Was it Asteria?' His eye fell on the paper.

'What's all this?' he said. 'Thomas Spinach? That's only me. My subconsciousness said it was Asparagus once.'

'But look what it has been writing,' said Sylvia.

He read it.

'That's queer,' he said. 'That can't be me. I'm not very unhappy. I don't want my own help. I know who I am.'

He jumped up.

'Most interesting,' he said. 'It looks like a new control. Young Spinach must be powerful, too; he came through the first time he tried. We'll investigate this, Sylvia. It would be fine to get a new control for our séances.'

'But not tonight, Ludovic,' said she. 'I really shouldn't sleep if you went on now. And he's violent. He made the loudest rap I ever heard.'

'Did he, indeed?' said Ludovic. 'I must have been in deep trance then, for I never heard it. We'll certainly try to snap him with the camera tomorrow.'

The morning was bright and sunny, and directly after breakfast Ludovic set to work with his photography. The first three or four films showed nothing but impenetrable blackness, and a consultation of his handbook convinced him that they must have been overexposed. He corrected this, and after a few errors on the other side, produced a negative which quite clearly showed Sylvia sitting by the long window into the verandah. This, though it revealed no 'extra', was an encouraging achievement, and he took half a dozen more exposures, with which he hurried away into the small dark cupboard under the stairs, where he had installed his developing and fixing baths. Shortly afterwards Sylvia heard her name called in crowing, exultant tones, and ran to see what had happened.

'Don't open the door,' he called, 'or you'll spoil it. But I've got a picture of you with a magnificent extra – a face hanging in the air by your shoulder.'

'How lovely!' shouted Sylvia. 'Do be quick and fix it.'

There was no sort of doubt about it. There she sat by the window, and close by her was a strange, inexplicable face. So much could be seen from the negative, and when a print was taken of it the details were wonderfully clear. It was the face of a young man; his handsome features wore an expression of agonised entreaty.

'Poor boy!' said Sylvia sympathetically. 'So good-looking too; but somehow I don't like him.'

Then a brilliant idea struck her.

'Oh, Ludovic,' she said, 'is it young Spinach?'

He snatched the print from her.

'I must fix it,' he said, 'or it will be ruined. Of course it's young Spinach. Who else could it be, I should like to know? We'll find out more about him this evening. Fancy obtaining that the very first morning!'

They spent the afternoon on the beach, in order to get in an elevated frame of mind by contemplating the beauties of nature, and after a light supper, prepared for a double séance. Two hooks, so to speak, were baited for Spinach, for in one chair sat Sylvia, with pencil and paper, ready to take down his slightest word, and in another Ludovic, similarly equipped. They both let themselves sink into that drowsy and vacant condition which they knew to be favourable to communications from the unseen, but for a long time they neither of them got a bite. Then Ludovic heard the dash and clatter of his sister's pencil, suddenly beginning to write very rapidly, and this aroused in him disturbing feelings of envy and jealousy, for something was coming through to Sylvia and not to him.

This inharmonious emotion quite dissipated the tranquillity which was a *sine qua non* of the receptive state, and he got up to see what was coming through to her. Probably some mawkish rubbish from Violetta about Savonarola's sermons. But the moment he saw her paper he was thrilled to the marrow.

'Yes, I'm Thomas Spinach,' he read, 'and I'm very unhappy. I came and stood by you this morning when the man was photographing. I want you to help me. Oh, do help me! It's something I've forgotten, though it is so important. I want you to look everywhere and see if you can't find something very unusual, and tell them. It is somewhere here. It must be, because I put it there, and I hardly like to tell you what it is, because it's terrible . . . .'

The pencil stopped. Ludovic was wildly excited, and his jealousy of Sylvia was almost forgotten. After all, it was he who had taken Spinach's photograph . . . .

Sylvia's hand continued idle so long that Ludovic, in order to stir it into activity again, began to ask questions.

'Have you passed over, Spinach?' he said.

Her hand began to write in a swift and irritated manner. 'Of course I have,' it scribbled. 'Otherwise I should know where it was.'

'Used you to live here?' asked Ludovic. 'And when did you pass over?'

'Yes, I lived here,' came the answer. 'I passed over a week ago. Very suddenly. There was a thunderstorm that night, and I had just finished it all, and was in the garden cooling down, when lightning struck me, and when I came to – on this side, you understand – I couldn't remember where it was.'

'Where what was?' asked Ludovic. 'Do you mean the thing you had finished? What was it you had finished?'

The pencil seemed to give a loud squeak, as if it was a slate pencil.

'Oh, here it is again,' it wrote in trembling characters. 'I can't go on now. It's terrible. I'm so frightened. Please, please find it.'

Just as on the previous evening, there came an appalling rap somewhere on the wall close to him, and, seriously startled, Ludovic sprang up, and shook Sylvia into consciousness. Whoever this spirit was, it was not a good, kind, mild one like Asteria, who, whenever she rapped, did so very softly and pleasantly.

Sylvia yawned and stretched herself.

'Spinach?' she said, drowsily. 'Any Spinach?'

'Yes, dear, quantities,' said Ludovic.

'And what did he say? Oh, I went off deep then, Ludovic. I don't know what's been happening. Violetta isn't nearly so powerful. Such an odd feeling! Did I write all that?'

'Yes, in answer to some pretty good questions of mine,' he said. 'It's really wonderful. We're on the track of young Spinach, or, rather, he's on ours.'

Sylvia was reading her manuscript.

'"I passed over a week ago,"' she said. '"Very suddenly – there was a thunderstorm that night – " Why, Ludovic, there was! That's quite true. You slept through it, but I didn't, and I remember reading in the paper that it had been very violent in the Rye district. How strange!'

Ludovic clicked his fingers.

'I know what I'll do,' he said. 'I shall send a telegram to Mrs Sapson. Give me a piece of paper. She said that wonderful visitors might perhaps come to me here.'

Sylvia grasped his thoughts.

'I see!' she cried. 'You mean to tell her that her late tenant, young Thomas Spinach, who was killed by lightning last week, has communicated with us. That will impress her tremendously, if you think she's had enough of Asteria. Indeed, I shouldn't wonder if she lent us this cottage just in order to test us, and see if we really received messages from the other side. What a score!'

She hastily scribbled on a leaf of her writing-block, counting up the words on her fingers. Her economical mind exerted itself to contrive the message in exactly twelve words.

'There!' she read out triumphantly. 'Listen! "Sapson, 29 Brompton Avenue, London. Tenant Spinach killed last week, thunderstorm, communicated." Just twelve. You needn't sign it, as it will have the Rye postmark.'

'My dear,' said he, 'it's no time for such petty economies. Better spend a few pence more and make it impressive and rather more intelligible. Give me some paper; I asked you before. And we must make it clear that it's not a chance word of local gossip that has inspired it. I shall tell her about the photograph too.'

Before they went to bed, Ludovic composed a more explicit telegram, and in the course of the next morning he received an enthusiastic reply from Mrs Sapson.

> ALL QUITE CORRECT AND MOST WONDERFUL [*she wrote*]. DELIGHTED YOU HAVE GOT INTO COMMUNICATION. FIND OUT MORE, AND ASK HIM ABOUT HIS UNCLE. WIRE AGAIN IF FRESH REVELATIONS OCCUR.

In order to secure themselves from the possibility of interruption, Sylvia gave Gramsby an afternoon out, which she proposed to spend in the excitements of Rye, and as soon as she was gone the mediums prepared for a séance. As Spinach seemed to fancy Sylvia, she composed herself for the trance-condition, with pencil and paper handy, and Ludovic sat by to ask questions. Very soon Sylvia's eyes closed, her head fell forward, and the pencil she held began to tremble violently, like a motor-car ready to start.

'Are you Spinach?' asked Ludovic, observing these signs of possession. Instantly the pencil began to write.

'Yes. Have you found it?'

'We don't know what it is,' said Ludovic. Then he remembered Mrs Sapson's telegram. 'Has it anything to do with your uncle?' he asked.

There was a long pause. Then the pencil began to move again.

'Please find him,' it wrote.

'But how are we to find your uncle?' asked Ludovic. 'We don't know where to look or what he's like. Tell us where to look.'

The pencil moved in a most agitated fashion.

'I don't know,' it wrote. 'If I knew I would tell you. But it's somewhere about. I had just put it somewhere, when the lightning came and killed me, and I can't remember. My memory's gone like – like after concussion of the brain.'

An uneasy thought struck Ludovic. Why did young Spinach allude to his uncle as 'it'?

'Is your uncle dead?' he asked. 'Is it his body that you mean by "it"?'

Sylvia's fingers writhed as if in mortal agony. Then the pencil jerked out, 'Yes.'

Ludovic, accustomed as he was to spirits, felt an icy shudder run through him. But he waited in silence, for the pencil looked as if it had something more to write. Then – great heavens – it came.

'I will tell you all,' it wrote. 'I killed him, and I can't remember where I put him.'

A spasm of moral indignation seized Ludovic.

'That was very wrong of you,' he justly observed. 'But we'll try to help you if you will tell us all about it. Come; you're dead. Nobody can hang you.'

Shocked as Ludovic was, and extremely uneasy also at the thought of the proximity not only of the spirit of a murderer, but the corpse of young Spinach's uncle, it was only natural that he should feel an overwhelming professional interest in the revelations that appeared to be imminent. It would be a glorious thing for his career to receive from a departed spirit the first-hand account of this undetected crime, and to be able to corroborate it by the discovery of the corpse. Though he had come down here for a holiday, the chance of such a unique piece of work made him feel quite rested already, for it was impossible to conceive a more magnificent advertisement. What a wonderful confirmation it would be also to Mrs Sapson's wavering faith in his psychical powers. She would publish the news of it far and wide, and the séances would be more popular than ever. Moreover, there was the chance of learning all sorts of fresh information about the conditions that prevailed on the other side, of a far more sensational and exciting quality than the method of the production of thought-flowers and flowing robes and general love and helpfulness . . . . He waited with the intensest expectation for anything that Spinach might vouchsafe.

At last it began, and now there was no need for further questions, for the pencil streamed across the page. Sheet after sheet of the writing-block was filled, and twice Ludovic had to sharpen Sylvia's pencil, for the point was quite worn down with these remarkable disclosures, and only made illegible scratches on the paper. For half an hour it careered over the sheets; then finally it made a great scrawl, and Sylvia's hand dropped inert. She stretched and yawned, and came to herself.

The next hour was the most absorbing that Ludovic had ever spent in his professional work. Together they read the account of the crime. Alexander Spinach, the uncle, was the most wicked of elderly gentlemen, who made his nephew's life an intolerable burden to him. He had found out that the orphan boy had committed a petty forgery with regard to a cheque which he had signed with his uncle's name, and, holding exposure and arrest over his head, had made him work for him day and night, fishing and farming and doing the work of the house without a penny-piece of wages, while he himself boozed his days away in the chimney-corner.

Long brooding over his wrongs and the misery of his life made young Spinach (very properly, as he still thought) determine to kill the odious old wretch, and he adroitly poisoned his whisky with weed-killer. He went out to his work next morning as usual, leaving the corpse in the locked-up house, and casually mentioned to the folk he came across that his uncle had gone up to London and would probably not be back for some time. When he returned in the evening he hid the body somewhere, meaning to dig a handsome excavation in the garden, and having buried it, plant some useful vegetables above it. But hardly had he made this temporary disposition of the corpse, than he was struck by lightning in the terrific storm that visited the district a week ago, and killed. When he came to himself on the spiritual plane he could not remember what he had done with the body.

So far the story was ordinary enough, apart from the interest in the manner of its communication, but now came that part of the confession which these ardent young psychicists saw would be a veritable gold-mine to them. For on emerging on the other side young Spinach found himself terrifyingly haunted not by the spirit, but by the body of his uncle. Just as on the material plane, so he explained, murderers are sometimes haunted by the spirit of their victim, so on the spiritual plane, quite logically, they may be haunted by the body of their victim. His uncle's bodily and palpable presence grimly pursued him wherever he went; even as he gathered sweet thought-flowers or thought-fruits, the terrible body appeared. If he woke at night he found it watching by his bed, if he bathed in the crystal rivers it swam beside him, and he had learned that he could never find peace till it was given proper burial. No doubt, he said, Ludovic had heard of the skeletons of murdered folk being walled up in secret chambers, and how their spirits haunted the place till their bones were discovered and interred. The converse was true on the other side, and while murdered corpses lay about unburied in the material world, their bodies haunted the perpetrator of the crime.

It was here that poor young Spinach's difficulty came in. The sudden lightning-stroke had bereft him of all memory of what he was doing just before, and, puzzle as he might, he could not recollect where he had put the corpse . . . . Then he broke out into passionate entreaties: 'Help me, help me, kind mediums,' he wrote. 'I know it is somewhere about, so search for it and get it buried. He was an awful old man and I can't describe the agony of being haunted by his beastly body. Find it and have it buried, and then I shall be free from its dreadful presence.'

They read this unique document together by the fading light, strung up to the highest pitch of professional interest, and yet peering awfully round from time to time in vague apprehension of what might happen next. During the séance the wind had got up, and now it was moaning round the corners of the house, and dusk was falling rapidly, with prospects of a wild night to follow. The curtains bulged and bellied in the draught, hollow voices sounded in the chimney, and Sylvia clung to her brother.

'I don't like it,' she wailed. 'I don't like this spirit of Spinach; Violetta and Asteria are far preferable. And then there's "It". It is somewhere about, and it may be anywhere.'

Ludovic made an attempt at gaiety.

'It may be anywhere, as you say,' he remarked, 'but it actually is somewhere. And we've got to find it, dear. Better find it before it gets dark. And think of the sensation there will be when we publish the account of how, in answer to the entreaty of a remorseful spirit – '

'But he isn't remorseful,' said Sylvia. 'There's not a word of remorse, but only terror at being haunted. There's not only a corpse about, but the spirit of an unrepentant murderer. It isn't pleasant. I would sooner be in expensive lodgings than here.'

'Oh, nonsense,' said Ludovic. 'Besides, young Spinach is friendly enough to us. We're his one hope. And if we find it he will certainly be very grateful. I shouldn't wonder if he sent us many more revelations. Even as it is, how deeply interesting! Nobody ever guessed that there were material ghosts in the spiritual world. But now we must get busy and search for Alexander. Fix your mind on what a tremendously paying experience this will be. Now, where shall we begin? There's the house and the garden – '

'Oh, I hope it will be in the garden,' said Sylvia. 'But there's no chance of that, for he meant to bury it in the garden afterwards.'

'True. We'll begin with the house, then. Now most murderers bury the body under the floor of the kitchen, cover it with quicklime, and fill in with cement.'

'But he wouldn't have had time for that,' said Sylvia. 'Besides, this was to be only a temporary resting-place.'

'Perhaps he cut it up,' said Ludovic, 'and we shall find a piece here and a piece there.'

The search began. In the growing dusk, with the wild wind increasing to a gale, they annealed themselves for the gruesome business. They investigated the coal-cellar, they peered into housemaids' cupboards, and with quaking hearts examined the woodshed. Here there were signs that its contents had been disturbed, and the sight of an old boot peeping out from behind some logs nearly caused Sylvia to collapse. Then Ludovic got a ladder, and, climbing up to the roof, interrogated the water-tank, from the contents of which they had already drunk. But all their explorations were in vain; there was no sign of the corpse. For a nerve-racking hour they persevered, and a dismal idea occurred to Ludovic.

'It can't be a practical joke on the part of Spinach, can it?' he said. 'That would be in the worst possible taste. Good gracious, what's that?'

There came a loud tapping at the front door, and Sylvia hid her face on his shoulder.

'That's Spinach,' she whispered. 'That terrible Spinach!'

They tottered to the door and opened it. On the threshold was a man, who told them he was the carrier from Rye, and brought a note for Miss Byron.

'I'm going back in half an hour, miss,' he said, 'if there's any answer. A box, I understood.'

The note was from Gramsby, who, though unwilling to 'upset' them, declined to come back to the cottage. She had heard things, and she didn't like it, and she would be obliged if they would pack her box and send it in.

'The coward!' said Sylvia, trembling violently. 'She shan't have her box unless she comes to fetch it.'

They went back into the sitting-room, lit the fire, and made it as cheerful as they could with many candles. Their flames wagged ominously in the eddying draughts, and the two drew their chairs close to the hearth. By now the full fury of the gale was unloosed, the whole house shuddered at the blasts, doors creaked, curtains whispered, flurries of rain were flung against the windows, and strange noises and stirrings muttered in the chimney.

'I shall just get warm,' said Ludovic, 'and then go on with the search. I shan't know a moment's peace till I find it.'

'I shan't know a moment's peace when you do!' wailed Sylvia.

They were sitting in the fire almost, and suddenly something up the chimney caught Ludovic's eye.

'What's that?' he said.

He got a candle and held it up the chimney.

'It's a rope,' he said, 'tied round a staple in the wall.'

His look met hers, and read the answering horror there.

'I'm going to undo it,' he said. 'Step back, Sylvia.'

There was no need to say that, for she had already retreated to the farthest corner of the room. He pulled the rope off the staple and let it go.

There was a scrambling, shuffling noise from high up in the chimney, and in a cloud of soot 'It' fell, with a heavy thud, sprawling across the hearth.

They fled into the night; the carrier had only just got to the garden gate.

'Take us into Rye,' cried Ludovic. 'Take us to the police-station. Murder has been done!'

*

The account of these amazing events duly appeared in all the psychical papers and many others. Long queues of would-be sitters formed up for the Byron séances, in the hopes of getting fresh revelations from young Spinach. But from association with Asteria and Violetta he gradually became quite common-place, and only told them about thought-flowers and white robes.

In the Tube

'It's a convention,' said Anthony Carling cheerfully, 'and not a very convincing one. Time, indeed! There's no such thing as Time really; it has no actual existence. Time is nothing more than an infinitesimal point in eternity, just as space is an infinitesimal point in infinity. At the most, Time is a sort of tunnel through which we are accustomed to believe that we are travelling. There's a roar in our ears and a darkness in our eyes which makes it seem real to us. But before we came into the tunnel we existed for ever in an infinite sunlight, and after we have got through it we shall exist in an infinite sunlight again. So why should we bother ourselves about the confusion and noise and darkness which only encompass us for a moment?'

For a firm-rooted believer in such immeasurable ideas as these, which he punctuated with brisk application of the poker to the brave sparkle and glow of the fire, Anthony has a very pleasant appreciation of the measurable and the finite, and nobody with whom I have acquaintance has so keen a zest for life and its enjoyments as he. He had given us this evening an admirable dinner, had passed round a port beyond praise, and had illuminated the jolly hours with the light of his infectious optimism. Now the small company had melted away, and I was left with him over the fire in his study. Outside the tattoo of wind-driven sleet was audible on the window-panes, over-scoring now and again the flap of the flames on the open hearth, and the thought of the chilly blasts and the snow-covered pavement in Brompton Square, across which, to skidding taxicabs, the last of his other guests had scurried, made my position, resident here till tomorrow morning, the more delicately delightful. Above all there was this stimulating and suggestive companion, who, whether he talked of the great abstractions which were so intensely real and practical to him, or of the very remarkable experiences which he had encountered among these conventions of time and space, was equally fascinating to the listener.

'I adore life,' he said. 'I find it the most entrancing plaything. It's a delightful game, and, as you know very well, the only conceivable way to play a game is to treat it extremely seriously. If you say to yourself, "It's only a game", you cease to take the slightest interest in it. You have to know that it's only a game, and behave as if it was the one object of existence. I should like it to go on for many years yet. But all the time one has to be living on the true plane as well, which is eternity and infinity. If you come to think of it, the one thing which the human mind cannot grasp is the finite, not the infinite, the temporary, not the eternal.'

'That sounds rather paradoxical,' said I.

'Only because you've made a habit of thinking about things that seem bounded and limited. Look it in the face for a minute. Try to imagine finite Time and Space, and you find you can't. Go back a million years, and multiply that million of years by another million, and you find that you can't conceive of a beginning. What happened before that beginning? Another beginning and another beginning? And before that? Look at it like that, and you find that the only solution comprehensible to you is the existence of an eternity, something that never began and will never end. It's the same about space. Project yourself to the farthest star, and what comes beyond that? Emptiness? Go on through the emptiness, and you can't imagine it being finite and having an end. It must needs go on for ever: that's the only thing you can understand. There's no such thing as before or after, or beginning or end, and what a comfort that is! I should fidget myself to death if there wasn't the huge soft cushion of eternity to lean one's head against. Some people say – I believe I've heard you say it yourself – that the idea of eternity is so tiring; you feel that you want to stop. But that's because you are thinking of eternity in terms of Time, and mumbling in your brain, "And after that, and after that?" Don't you grasp the idea that in eternity there isn't any "after", any more than there is any "before"? It's all one. Eternity isn't quantity: it's a quality.'

Sometimes, when Anthony talks in this manner, I seem to get a glimpse of that which to his mind is so transparently clear and solidly real, at other times (not having a brain that readily envisages abstractions) I feel as though he was pushing me over a precipice, and my intellectual faculties grasp wildly at anything tangible or comprehensible. This was the case now, and I hastily interrupted.

'But there is a "before" and "after", ' I said. 'A few hours ago you gave us an admirable dinner, and after that – yes, after – we played bridge. And now you are going to explain things a little more clearly to me, and after that I shall go to bed – '

He laughed.

'You shall do exactly as you like,' he said, 'and you shan't be a slave to Time either tonight or tomorrow morning. We won't even mention an hour for breakfast, but you shall have it in eternity whenever you awake. And as I see it is not midnight yet, we'll slip the bonds of Time, and talk quite infinitely. I will stop the clock, if that will assist you in getting rid of your illusion, and then I'll tell you a story, which to my mind, shows how unreal so-called realities are; or, at any rate, how fallacious are our senses as judges of what is real and what is not.'

'Something occult, something spookish?' I asked, pricking up my ears, for Anthony has the strangest clairvoyances and visions of things unseen by the normal eye.

'I suppose you might call some of it occult,' he said, 'though there's a certain amount of rather grim reality mixed up in it.'

'Go on; excellent mixture,' said I.

He threw a fresh log on the fire.

'It's a longish story,' he said. 'You may stop me as soon as you've had enough. But there will come a point for which I claim your consideration. You, who cling to your "before" and "after", has it ever occurred to you how difficult it is to say *when* an incident takes place? Say that a man commits some crime of violence, can we not, with a good deal of truth, say that he really commits that crime when he definitely plans and determines upon it, dwelling on it with gusto? The actual commission of it, I think we can reasonably argue, is the mere material sequel of his resolve: he is guilty of it when he makes that determination. When, therefore, in the term of "before" and "after", does the crime truly take place? There is also in my story a further point for your consideration. For it seems certain that the spirit of a man, after the death of his body, is obliged to re-enact such a crime, with a view, I suppose we may guess, to his remorse and his eventual redemption. Those who have second sight have seen such re-enactments. Perhaps he may have done his deed blindly in this life; but then his spirit re-commits it with its spiritual eyes open, and able to comprehend its enormity. So, shall we view the man's original determination and the material commission of his crime only as preludes to the real commission of it, when with eyes unsealed he does it and repents of it? . . . . That all sounds very obscure when I speak in the abstract, but I think you will see what I mean, if you follow my tale. Comfortable? Got everything you want? Here goes, then.'

He leaned back in his chair, concentrating his mind, and then spoke.

'The story that I am about to tell you,' he said, 'had its beginning a month ago, when you were away in Switzerland. It reached its conclusion, so I imagine, last night. I do not, at any rate, expect to experience any more of it. Well, a month ago I was returning late on a very wet night from dining out. There was not a taxi to be had, and I hurried through the pouring rain to the tube-station at Piccadilly Circus, and thought myself very lucky to catch the last train in this direction. The carriage into which I stepped was quite empty except for one other passenger, who sat next the door immediately opposite to me. I had never, to my knowledge, seen him before, but I found my attention vividly fixed on him, as if he somehow concerned me. He was a man of middle age, in dress-clothes, and his face wore an expression of intense thought, as if in his mind he was pondering some very significant matter, and his hand which was resting on his knee clenched and unclenched itself. Suddenly he looked up and stared me in the face, and I saw there suspicion and fear, as if I had surprised him in some secret deed.

'At that moment we stopped at Dover Street, and the conductor threw open the doors, announced the station and added, "Change here for Hyde Park Corner and Gloucester Road." That was all right for me since it meant that the train would stop at Brompton Road, which was my destination. It was all right apparently, too, for my companion, for he certainly did not get out, and after a moment's stop, during which no one else got in, we went on. I saw him, I must insist, after the doors were closed and the train had started. But when I looked again, as we rattled on, I saw that there was no one there. I was quite alone in the carriage.

'Now you may think that I had had one of those swift momentary dreams which flash in and out of the mind in the space of a second, but I did not believe it was so myself, for I felt that I had experienced some sort of premonition or clairvoyant vision. A man, the semblance of whom, astral body or whatever you may choose to call it, I had just seen, would sometime sit in that seat opposite to me, pondering and planning.'

'But why?' I asked. 'Why should it have been the astral body of a living man which you thought you had seen? Why not the ghost of a dead one?'

'Because of my own sensations. The sight of the spirit of someone dead, which has occurred to me two or three times in my life, has always been accompanied by a physical shrinking and fear, and by the sensation of cold and of loneliness. I believed, at any rate, that I had seen a phantom of the living, and that impression was confirmed, I might say proved, the next day. For I met the man himself. And the next night, as you shall hear, I met the phantom again. We will take them in order.

'I was lunching, then, the next day with my neighbour Mrs Stanley: there was a small party, and when I arrived we waited but for the final guest. He entered while I was talking to some friend, and presently at my elbow I heard Mrs Stanley's voice –

' "Let me introduce you to Sir Henry Payle," she said.

'I turned and saw my *vis-à-vis* of the night before. It was quite unmistakably he, and as we shook hands he looked at me I thought with vague and puzzled recognition.

' "Haven't we met before, Mr Carling?" he said. "I seem to recollect – "

'For the moment I forgot the strange manner of his disappearance from the carriage, and thought that it had been the man himself whom I had seen last night.

' "Surely, and not so long ago," I said. "For we sat opposite each other in the last tube-train from Piccadilly Circus yesterday night."

'He still looked at me, frowning, puzzled, and shook his head.

' "That can hardly be," he said. "I only came up from the country this morning."

'Now this interested me profoundly, for the astral body, we are told, abides in some half-conscious region of the mind or spirit, and has recollections of what has happened to it, which it can convey only very vaguely and dimly to the conscious mind. All lunch-time I could see his eyes again and again directed to me with the same puzzled and perplexed air, and as I was taking my departure he came up to me.

'"I shall recollect some day," he said, "where we met before, and I hope we may meet again. Was it not – ?" and he stopped. "No: it has gone from me," he added.'

The log that Anthony had thrown on the fire was burning bravely now, and its high-flickering flame lit up his face.

'Now, I don't know whether you believe in coincidences as chance things,' he said, 'but if you do, get rid of the notion. Or if you can't at once, call it a coincidence that that very night I again caught the last train on the tube going westwards. This time, so far from my being a solitary passenger, there was a considerable crowd waiting at Dover Street, where I entered, and just as the noise of the approaching train began to reverberate in the tunnel I caught sight of Sir Henry Payle standing near the opening from which the train would presently emerge, apart from the rest of the crowd. And I thought to myself how odd it was that I should have seen the phantom of him at this very hour last night and the man himself now, and I began walking towards him with the idea of saying, "Anyhow, it is in the tube that we meet tonight." . . . And then a terrible and awful thing happened. Just as the train emerged from the tunnel he jumped down on to the line in front of it, and the train swept along over him up the platform.

'For a moment I was stricken with horror at the sight, and I remember covering my eyes against the dreadful tragedy. But then I perceived that, though it had taken place in full sight of those who were waiting, no one seemed to have seen it except myself. The driver, looking out from his window, had not applied his brakes, there was no jolt from the advancing train, no scream, no cry, and the rest of the passengers began boarding the train with perfect nonchalance. I must have staggered, for I felt sick and faint with what I had seen, and some kindly soul put his arm round me and supported me into the train. He was a doctor, he told me, and asked if I was in pain, or what ailed me. I told him what I thought I had seen, and he assured me that no such accident had taken place.

'It was clear then to my own mind that I had seen the second act, so to speak, in this psychical drama, and I pondered next morning over the problem as to what I should do. Already I had glanced at the morning paper, which, as I knew would be the case, contained no mention whatever of what I had seen. The thing had certainly not happened, but I knew in myself that it would happen. The flimsy veil of Time had been withdrawn from my eyes, and I had seen into what you would call the future. In terms of Time of course it was the future, but from my point of view the thing was just as much in the past as it was in the future. It existed, and waited only for its material fulfilment. The more I thought about it, the more I saw that I could do nothing.'

I interrupted his narrative.

'You did nothing?' I exclaimed. 'Surely you might have taken some step in order to try to avert the tragedy.'

He shook his head.

'What step precisely?' he said. 'Was I to go to Sir Henry and tell him that once more I had seen him in the tube in the act of committing suicide? Look at it like this. Either what I had seen was pure illusion, pure imagination, in which case it had no existence or significance at all, or it was actual and real, and essentially it had happened. Or take it, though not very logically, somewhere between the two. Say that the idea of suicide, for some cause of which I knew nothing, had occurred to him or would occur. Should I not, if that was the case, be doing a very dangerous thing, by making such a suggestion to him? Might not the fact of my telling him what I had seen put the idea into his mind, or, if it was already there, confirm it and strengthen it? "It's a ticklish matter to play with souls," as Browning says.'

'But it seems so inhuman not to interfere in any way,' said I, 'not to make any attempt.'

'What interference?' asked he. 'What attempt?'

The human instinct in me still seemed to cry aloud at the thought of doing nothing to avert such a tragedy, but it seemed to be beating itself against something austere and inexorable. And cudgel my brain as I would, I could not combat the sense of what he had said. I had no answer for him, and he went on.

'You must recollect, too,' he said, 'that I believed then and believe now that the thing had happened. The cause of it, whatever that was, had begun to work, and the effect, in this material sphere, was inevitable. That is what I alluded to when, at the beginning of my story, I asked you to consider how difficult it was to say when an action took place. You still hold that this particular action, this suicide of Sir Henry, had not yet taken place, because he had not yet thrown himself under the advancing train. To me that seems a materialistic view. I hold that in all but the endorsement of it, so to speak, it had taken place. I fancy that Sir Henry, for instance, now free from the material dusks, knows that himself.'

Exactly as he spoke there swept through the warm lit room a current of ice-cold air, ruffling my hair as it passed me, and making the wood flames on the hearth to dwindle and flare. I looked round to see if the door at my back had opened, but nothing stirred there, and over the closed window the curtains were fully drawn. As it reached Anthony, he sat up quickly in his chair and directed his glance this way and that about the room.

'Did you feel that?' he asked.

'Yes: a sudden draught,' I said. 'Ice-cold.'

'Anything else?' he asked. 'Any other sensation?'

I paused before I answered, for at the moment there occurred to me Anthony's differentiation of the effects produced on the beholder by a phantasm of the living and the apparition of the dead. It was the latter which accurately described my sensations now, a certain physical shrinking, a fear, a feeling of desolation. But yet I had seen nothing. 'I felt rather creepy,' I said.

As I spoke I drew my chair rather closer to the fire, and sent a swift and, I confess, a somewhat apprehensive scrutiny round the walls of the brightly lit room. I noticed at the same time that Anthony was peering across to the chimney-piece, on which, just below a sconce holding two electric lights, stood the clock which at the beginning of our talk he had offered to stop. The hands I noticed pointed to twenty-five minutes to one.

'But you saw nothing?' he asked.

'Nothing whatever,' I said. 'Why should I? What was there to see? Or did you – '

'I don't think so,' he said.

Somehow this answer got on my nerves, for the queer feeling which had accompanied that cold current of air had not left me. If anything it had become more acute.

'But surely you know whether you saw anything or not?' I said.

'One can't always be certain,' said he. 'I say that I don't think I saw anything. But I'm not sure, either, whether the story I am telling you was quite concluded last night. I think there may be a further incident. If you prefer it, I will leave the rest of it, as far as I know it, unfinished till tomorrow morning, and you can go off to bed now.'

His complete calmness and tranquillity reassured me.

'But why should I do that?' I asked.

Again he looked round on the bright walls.

'Well, I think something entered the room just now,' he said, 'and it may develop. If you don't like the notion, you had better go. Of course there's nothing to be alarmed at; whatever it is, it can't hurt us. But it is close on the hour when on two successive nights I saw what I have already told you, and an apparition usually occurs at the same time. Why that is so, I cannot say, but certainly it looks as if a spirit that is earth-bound is still subject to certain conventions, the conventions of time for instance. I think that personally I shall see something before long, but most likely you won't. You're not such a sufferer as I from these – these delusions – '

I was frightened and knew it, but I was also intensely interested, and some perverse pride wriggled within me at his last words. Why, so I asked myself, shouldn't I see whatever was to be seen? . . . .

'I don't want to go in the least,' I said. 'I want to hear the rest of your story.'

'Where was I, then? Ah, yes: you were wondering why I didn't do something after I saw the train move up to the platform, and I said that there was nothing to be done. If you think it over, I fancy you will agree with me . . . . A couple of days passed, and on the third morning I saw in the paper that there had come fulfilment to my vision. Sir Henry Payle, who had been waiting on the platform of Dover Street Station for the last train to South Kensington, had thrown himself in front of it as it came into the station. The train had been pulled up in a couple of yards, but a wheel had passed over his chest, crushing it in and instantly killing him.

'An inquest was held, and there emerged at it one of those dark stories which, on occasions like these, sometimes fall like a midnight shadow across a life that the world perhaps had thought prosperous. He had long been on bad terms with his wife, from whom he had lived apart, and it appeared that not long before this he had fallen desperately in love with another woman. The night before his suicide he had appeared very late at his wife's house, and had a long and angry scene with her in which he entreated her to divorce him, threatening otherwise to make her life a hell to her. She refused, and in an ungovernable fit of passion he attempted to strangle her. There was a struggle and the noise of it caused her manservant to come up, who succeeded in overmastering him. Lady Payle threatened to proceed against him for assault with the intention to murder her. With this hanging over his head, the next night, as I have already told you, he committed suicide.'

He glanced at the clock again, and I saw that the hands now pointed to ten minutes to one. The fire was beginning to burn low and the room surely was growing strangely cold.

'That's not quite all,' said Anthony, again looking round. 'Are you sure you wouldn't prefer to hear it tomorrow?'

The mixture of shame and pride and curiosity again prevailed.

'No: tell me the rest of it at once,' I said.

Before speaking, he peered suddenly at some point behind my chair, shading his eyes. I followed his glance, and knew what he meant by saying that sometimes one could not be sure whether one saw something or not. But was that an outlined shadow that intervened between me and the wall? It was difficult to focus; I did not know whether it was near the wall or near my chair. It seemed to clear away, anyhow, as I looked more closely at it.

'You see nothing?' asked Anthony.

'No: I don't think so,' said I. 'And you?'

'I think I do,' he said, and his eyes followed something which was invisible to mine. They came to rest between him and the chimney-piece. Looking steadily there, he spoke again.

'All this happened some weeks ago,' he said, 'when you were out in Switzerland, and since then, up till last night, I saw nothing further. But all the time I was expecting something further. I felt that, as far as I was concerned, it was not all over yet, and last night, with the intention of assisting any communication to come through to me from – from beyond, I went into the Dover Street tube-station at a few minutes before one o'clock, the hour at which both the assault and the suicide had taken place. The platform when I arrived on it was absolutely empty, or appeared to be so, but presently, just as I began to hear the roar of the approaching train, I saw there was the figure of a man standing some twenty yards from me, looking into the tunnel. He had not come down with me in the lift, and the moment before he had not been there. He began moving towards me, and then I saw who it was, and I felt a stir of wind icy-cold coming towards me as he approached. It was not the draught that heralds the approach of a train, for it came from the opposite direction. He came close up to me, and I saw there was recognition in his eyes. He raised his face towards me and I saw his lips move, but, perhaps in the increasing noise from the tunnel, I heard nothing come from them. He put out his hand, as if entreating me to do something, and with a cowardice for which I cannot forgive myself, I shrank from him, for I knew, by the sign that I have told you, that this was one from the dead, and my flesh quaked before him, drowning for the moment all pity and all desire to help him, if that was possible. Certainly he had something which he wanted of me, but I recoiled from him. And by now the train was emerging from the tunnel, and next moment, with a dreadful gesture of despair, he threw himself in front of it.'

As he finished speaking he got up quickly from his chair, still looking fixedly in front of him. I saw his pupils dilate, and his mouth worked.

'It is coming,' he said. 'I am to be given a chance of atoning for my cowardice. There is nothing to be afraid of: I must remember that myself . . . .'

As he spoke there came from the panelling above the chimney-piece one loud shattering crack, and the cold wind again circled about my head. I found myself shrinking back in my chair with my hands held in front of me as instinctively I screened myself against something which I knew was there but which I could not see. Every sense told me that there was a presence in the room other than mine and Anthony's, and the horror of it was that I could not see it. Any vision, however terrible, would, I felt, be more tolerable than this clear certain knowledge that close to me was this invisible thing. And yet what horror might not be disclosed of the face of the dead and the crushed chest . . . . But all I could see, as I shuddered in this cold wind, was the familiar walls of the room, and Anthony standing in front of me stiff and firm, making, as I knew, a call on his courage. His eyes were focused on something quite close to him, and some semblance of a smile quivered on his mouth. And then he spoke again.

'Yes, I know you,' he said. 'And you want something of me. Tell me, then, what it is.'

There was absolute silence, but what was silence to my ears could not have been so to his, for once or twice he nodded, and once he said, 'Yes: I see. I will do it.' And with the knowledge that, even as there was someone here whom I could not see, so there was speech going on which I could not hear, this terror of the dead and of the unknown rose in me with the sense of powerlessness to move that accompanies nightmare. I could not stir, I could not speak. I could only strain my ears for the inaudible and my eyes for the unseen, while the cold wind from the very valley of the shadow of death streamed over me. It was not that the presence of death itself was terrible; it was that from its tranquillity and serene keeping there had been driven some unquiet soul unable to rest in peace for whatever ultimate awakening rouses the countless generations of those who have passed away, driven, no less, from whatever activities are theirs, back into the material world from which it should have been delivered. Never, until the gulf between the living and the dead was thus bridged, had it seemed so immense and so unnatural. It is possible that the dead may have communication with the living, and it was not that exactly that so terrified me, for such communication, as we know it, comes voluntarily from them. But here was something icy-cold and crime-laden, that was chased back from the peace that would not pacify it.

And then, most horrible of all, there came a change in these unseen conditions. Anthony was silent now, and from looking straight and fixedly in front of him, he began to glance sideways to where I sat and back again, and with that I felt that the unseen presence had turned its attention from him to me. And now, too, gradually and by awful degrees I began to see . . . .

There came an outline of shadow across the chimney-piece and the panels above it. It took shape: it fashioned itself into the outline of a man. Within the shape of the shadow details began to form themselves, and I saw wavering in the air, like something concealed by haze, the semblance of a face, stricken and tragic, and burdened with such a weight of woe as no human face had ever worn. Next, the shoulders outlined themselves, and a stain livid and red spread out below them, and suddenly the vision leaped into clearness. There he stood, the chest crushed in and drowned in the red stain, from which broken ribs, like the bones of a wrecked ship, protruded. The mournful, terrible eyes were fixed on me, and it was from them, so I knew, that the bitter wind proceeded . . . .

Then, quick as the switching off of a lamp, the spectre vanished, and the bitter wind was still, and opposite to me stood Anthony, in a quiet, bright-lit room. There was no sense of an unseen presence any more; he and I were then alone, with an interrupted conversation still dangling between us in the warm air. I came round to that, as one comes round after an anaesthetic. It all swam into sight again, unreal at first, and gradually assuming the texture of actuality.

'You were talking to somebody, not to me,' I said. 'Who was it? What was it?'

He passed the back of his hand over his forehead, which glistened in the light.

'A soul in hell,' he said.

Now it is hard ever to recall mere physical sensations, when they have passed. If you have been cold and are warmed, it is difficult to remember what cold was like: if you have been hot and have got cool, it is difficult to realise what the oppression of heat really meant. Just so, with the passing of that presence, I found myself unable to recapture the sense of the terror with which, a few moments ago only, it had invaded and inspired me.

'A soul in hell?' I said. 'What are you talking about?'

He moved about the room for a minute or so, and then came and sat on the arm of my chair.

'I don't know what you saw,' he said, 'or what you felt, but there has never in all my life happened to me anything more real than what these last few minutes have brought. I have talked to a soul in the hell of remorse, which is the only possible hell. He knew, from what happened last night, that he could perhaps establish communication through me with the world he had quitted, and he sought me and found me. I am charged with a mission to a woman I have never seen, a message from the contrite . . . . You can guess who it is . . . .'

He got up with a sudden briskness.

'Let's verify it anyhow,' he said. 'He gave me the street and the number. Ah, there's the telephone book! Would it be a coincidence merely if I found that at No. 20 in Chasemore Street, South Kensington, there lived a Lady Payle?'

He turned over the leaves of the bulky volume.

'Yes, that's right,' he said.

The Man Who Went Too Far

The little village of St Faith's nestles in a hollow of wooded hill up on the north bank of the river Fawn in the country of Hampshire, huddling close round its grey Norman church as if for spiritual protection against the fays and fairies, the trolls and 'little people', who might be supposed still to linger in the vast empty spaces of the New Forest, and to come after dusk and do their doubtful businesses. Once outside the hamlet you may walk in any direction (so long as you avoid the high road which leads to Brockenhurst) for the length of a summer afternoon without seeing sign of human habitation, or possibly even catching sight of another human being. Shaggy wild ponies may stop their feeding for a moment as you pass, the white scuts of rabbits will vanish into their burrows, a brown viper perhaps will glide from your path into a clump of heather, and unseen birds will chuckle in the bushes, but it may easily happen that for a long day you will see nothing human. But you will not feel in the least lonely; in summer, at any rate, the sunlight will be gay with butterflies, and the air thick with all those woodland sounds which like instruments in an orchestra combine to play the great symphony of the yearly festival of June. Winds whisper in the birches, and sigh among the firs; bees are busy with their redolent labour among the heather, a myriad birds chirp in the green temples of the forest trees, and the voice of the river prattling over stony places, bubbling into pools, chuckling and gulping round corners, gives you the sense that many presences and companions are near at hand.

Yet, oddly enough, though one would have thought that these benign and cheerful influences of wholesome air and spaciousness of forest were very healthful comrades for a man, in so far as Nature can really influence this wonderful human genus which has in these centuries learned to defy her most violent storms in its well-established houses, to bridle her torrents and make them light its streets, to tunnel her mountains and plough her seas, the inhabitants of St Faith's will not willingly venture into the forest after dark. For in spite of the silence and loneliness of the hooded night it seems that a man is not sure in what company he may suddenly find himself, and though it is difficult to get from these villagers any very clear story of occult appearances, the feeling is widespread. One story indeed I have heard with some definiteness, the tale of a monstrous goat that has been seen to skip with hellish glee about the woods and shady places, and this perhaps is connected with the story which I have here attempted to piece together. It too is well-known to them; for all remember the young artist who died here not long ago, a young man, or so he struck the beholder, of great personal beauty, with something about him that made men's faces to smile and brighten when they looked on him. His ghost they will tell you 'walks' constantly by the stream and through the woods which he loved so, and in especial it haunts a certain house, the last of the village, where he lived, and its garden in which he was done to death. For my part I am inclined to think that the terror of the Forest dates chiefly from that day. So, such as the story is, I have set it forth in connected form. It is based partly on the accounts of the villagers, but mainly on that of Darcy, a friend of mine and a friend of the man with whom these events were chiefly concerned.

The day had been one of untarnished midsummer splendour, and as the sun drew near to its setting, the glory of the evening grew every moment more crystalline, more miraculous. Westward from St Faith's the beechwood which stretched for some miles toward the heathery upland beyond already cast its veil of clear shadow over the red roofs of the village, but the spire of the grey church, overtopping all, still pointed a flaming orange finger into the sky. The river Fawn, which runs below, lay in sheets of sky-reflected blue, and wound its dreamy devious course round the edge of this wood, where a rough two-planked bridge crossed from the bottom of the garden of the last house in the village, and communicated by means of a little wicker gate with the wood itself. Then once out of the shadow of the wood the stream lay in flaming pools of the molten crimson of the sunset, and lost itself in the haze of woodland distances.

This house at the end of the village stood outside the shadow, and the lawn which sloped down to the river was still flecked with sunlight. Garden-beds of dazzling colour lined its gravel walks, and down the middle of it ran a brick pergola, half-hidden in clusters of rambler-rose and purple with starry clematis. At the bottom end of it, between two of its pillars, was slung a hammock containing a shirtsleeved figure.

The house itself lay somewhat remote from the rest of the village, and a footpath leading across two fields, now tall and fragrant with hay, was its only communication with the high road. It was low-built, only two storeys in height, and like the garden, its walls were a mass of flowering roses. A narrow stone terrace ran along the garden front, over which was stretched an awning, and on the terrace a young silent-footed man-servant was busied with the laying of the table for dinner. He was neat-handed and quick with his job, and having finished it he went back into the house, and reappeared again with a large rough bath-towel on his arm. With this he went to the hammock in the pergola.

'Nearly eight, sir,' he said.

'Has Mr Darcy come yet?' asked a voice from the hammock.

'No, sir.'

'If I'm not back when he comes, tell him that I'm just having a bathe before dinner.'

The servant went back to the house, and after a moment or two Frank Halton struggled to a sitting posture, and slipped out on to the grass. He was of medium height and rather slender in build, but the supple ease and grace of his movements gave the impression of great physical strength: even his descent from the hammock was not an awkward performance. His face and hands were of very dark complexion, either from constant exposure to wind and sun, or, as his black hair and dark eyes tended to show, from some strain of southern blood. His head was small, his face of an exquisite beauty of modelling, while the smoothness of its contour would have led you to believe that he was a beardless lad still in his teens. But something, some look which living and experience alone can give, seemed to contradict that, and finding yourself completely puzzled as to his age, you would next moment probably cease to think about that, and only look at this glorious specimen of young manhood with wondering satisfaction.

He was dressed as became the season and the heat, and wore only a shirt open at the neck, and a pair of flannel trousers. His head, covered very thickly with a somewhat rebellious crop of short curly hair, was bare as he strolled across the lawn to the bathing-place that lay below. Then for a moment there was silence, then the sound of splashed and divided waters, and presently after, a great shout of ecstatic joy, as he swam up-stream with the foamed water standing in a frill round his neck. Then after some five minutes of limb-stretching struggle with the flood, he turned over on his back, and with arms thrown wide, floated down-stream, ripple-cradled and inert. His eyes were shut, and between half-parted lips he talked gently to himself.

'I am one with it,' he said to himself, 'the river and I, I and the river. The coolness and splash of it is I, and the water-herbs that wave in it are I also. And my strength and my limbs are not mine but the river's. It is all one, all one, dear Fawn.'

A quarter of an hour later he appeared again at the bottom of the lawn, dressed as before, his wet hair already drying into its crisp short curls again. There he paused a moment, looking back at the stream with the smile with which men look on the face of a friend, then turned towards the house. Simultaneously his servant came to the door leading on to the terrace, followed by a man who appeared to be some half-way through the fourth decade of his years. Frank and he saw each other across the bushes and garden-beds, and each quickening his step, they met suddenly face to face round an angle of the garden walk, in the fragrance of syringa.

'My dear Darcy,' cried Frank, 'I am charmed to see you.'

But the other stared at him in amazement.

'Frank!' he exclaimed.

'Yes, that is my name,' he said, laughing; 'what is the matter?'

Darcy took his hand.

'What have you done to yourself?' he asked. 'You are a boy again.'

'Ah, I have a lot to tell you,' said Frank. 'Lots that you will hardly believe, but I shall convince you – '

He broke off suddenly, and held up his hand.

'Hush, there is my nightingale,' he said.

The smile of recognition and welcome with which he had greeted his friend faded from his face, and a look of rapt wonder took its place, as of a lover listening to the voice of his beloved. His mouth parted slightly, showing the white line of teeth, and his eyes looked out and out till they seemed to Darcy to be focused on things beyond the vision of man. Then something perhaps startled the bird, for the song ceased.

'Yes, lots to tell you,' he said. 'Really I am delighted to see you. But you look rather white and pulled down; no wonder after that fever. And there is to be no nonsense about this visit. It is June now, you stop here till you are fit to begin work again. Two months at least.'

'Ah, I can't trespass quite to that extent.'

Frank took his arm and walked him down the grass.

'Trespass? Who talks of trespass? I shall tell you quite openly when I am tired of you, but you know when we had the studio together, we used not to bore each other. However, it is ill talking of going away on the moment of your arrival. Just a stroll to the river, and then it will be dinner-time.'

Darcy took out his cigarette case, and offered it to the other.

Frank laughed.

'No, not for me. Dear me, I suppose I used to smoke once. How very odd!'

'Given it up?'

'I don't know. I suppose I must have. Anyhow I don't do it now. I would as soon think of eating meat.'

'Another victim on the smoking altar of vegetarianism?'

'Victim?' asked Frank. 'Do I strike you as such?'

He paused on the margin of the stream and whistled softly. Next moment a moor-hen made its splashing flight across the river, and ran up the bank. Frank took it very gently in his hands and stroked its head, as the creature lay against his shirt.

'And is the house among the reeds still secure?' he half-crooned to it. 'And is the missus quite well, and are the neighbours flourishing? There, dear, home with you,' and he flung it into the air.

'That bird's very tame,' said Darcy, slightly bewildered.

'It is rather,' said Frank, following its flight.

*

During dinner Frank chiefly occupied himself in bringing himself up to date in the movements and achievements of this old friend whom he had not seen for six years. Those six years, it now appeared, had been full of incident and success for Darcy; he had made a name for himself as a portrait painter which bade fair to outlast the vogue of a couple of seasons, and his leisure time had been brief. Then some four months previously he had been through a severe attack of typhoid, the result of which as concerns this story was that he had come down to this sequestered place to recruit.

'Yes, you've got on,' said Frank at the end. 'I always knew you would. A.R.A. with more in prospect. Money? You roll in it, I suppose, and, O Darcy, how much happiness have you had all these years? That is the only imperishable possession. And how much have you learned? Oh, I don't mean in Art. Even I could have done well in that.'

Darcy laughed.

'Done well? My dear fellow, all I have learned in these six years you knew, so to speak, in your cradle. Your old pictures fetch huge prices. Do you never paint now?'

Frank shook his head.

'No, I'm too busy,' he said.

'Doing what? Please tell me. That is what everyone is for ever asking me.'

'Doing? I suppose you would say I do nothing.'

Darcy glanced up at the brilliant young face opposite him.

'It seems to suit you, that way of being busy,' he said. 'Now, it's your turn. Do you read? Do you study? I remember you saying that it would do us all – all us artists, I mean – a great deal of good if we would study any one human face carefully for a year, without recording a line. Have you been doing that?'

Frank shook his head again.

'I mean exactly what I say,' he said. 'I have been *doing* nothing. And I have never been so occupied. Look at me; have I not done something to myself to begin with?'

'You are two years younger than I,' said Darcy, 'at least you used to be. You therefore are thirty-five. But had I never seen you before I should say you were just twenty. But was it worth while to spend six years of greatly-occupied life in order to look twenty? Seems rather like a woman of fashion.'

Frank laughed boisterously.

'First time I've ever been compared to that particular bird of prey,' he said. 'No, that has not been my occupation – in fact I am only very rarely conscious that one effect of my occupation has been that. Of course, it must have been if one comes to think of it. It is not very important. Quite true my body has become young. But that is very little; I have become young.'

Darcy pushed back his chair and sat sideways to the table looking at the other.

'Has that been your occupation then?' he asked.

'Yes, that anyhow is one aspect of it. Think what youth means! It is the capacity for growth; mind, body, spirit, all grow, all get stronger, all have a fuller, firmer life every day. That is something, considering that every day that passes after the ordinary man reaches the full-blown flower of his strength, weakens his hold on life. A man reaches his prime, and remains, we say, in his prime for ten years, or perhaps twenty. But after his primest prime is reached, he slowly, insensibly weakens. These are the signs of age in you, in your body, in your art probably, in your mind. You are less electric than you were. But I, when I reach my prime – I am nearing it – ah, you shall see.'

The stars had begun to appear in the blue velvet of the sky, and to the east the horizon seen above the black silhouette of the village was growing dove-coloured with the approach of moon-rise. White moths hovered dimly over the garden-beds, and the footsteps of night tip-toed through the bushes. Suddenly Frank rose.

'Ah, it is the supreme moment,' he said softly. 'Now more than at any other time the current of life, the eternal imperishable current runs so close to me that I am almost enveloped in it. Be silent a minute.'

He advanced to the edge of the terrace and looked out, standing stretched with arms outspread. Darcy heard him draw a long breath into his lungs, and after many seconds expel it again. Six or eight times he did this, then turned back into the lamplight.

'It will sound to you quite mad, I expect,' he said, 'but if you want to hear the soberest truth I have ever spoken and shall ever speak, I will tell you about myself. But come into the garden if it is not damp for you. I have never told anyone yet, but I shall like to tell you. It is long, in fact, since I have even tried to classify what I have learned.'

They wandered into the fragrant dimness of the pergola, and sat down. Then Frank began.

'Years ago, do you remember,' he said, 'we used often to talk about the decay of joy in the world. Many impulses, we settled, had contributed to this decay, some of which were good in themselves, others that were quite completely bad. Among the good things, I put what we may call certain Christian virtues, renunciation, resignation, sympathy with suffering, and the desire to relieve sufferers. But out of those things spring very bad ones, useless renunciation, asceticism for its own sake, mortification of the flesh with nothing to follow, no corresponding gain that is, and that awful and terrible disease which devastated England some centuries ago, and from which by heredity of spirit we suffer now, Puritanism. That was a dreadful plague, the brutes held and taught that joy and laughter and merriment were evil: it was a doctrine the most profane and wicked. Why, what is the commonest crime one sees? A sullen face. That is the truth of the matter.

'Now all my life I have believed that we are intended to be happy, that joy is of all gifts the most divine. And when I left London, abandoned my career, such as it was, I did so because I intended to devote my life to the cultivation of joy, and, by continuous and unsparing effort, to be happy. Among people, and in constant intercourse with others, I did not find it possible; there were too many distractions in towns and work-rooms, and also too much suffering. So I took one step backwards or forwards, as you may choose to put it, and went straight to Nature, to trees, birds, animals, to all those things which quite clearly pursue one aim only, which blindly follow the great native instinct to be happy without any care at all for morality, or human law or divine law. I wanted, you understand, to get all joy first-hand and unadulterated, and I think it scarcely exists among men; it is obsolete.'

Darcy turned in his chair.

'Ah, but what makes birds and animals happy?' he asked. 'Food, food and mating.'

Frank laughed gently in the stillness.

'Do not think I became a sensualist,' he said. 'I did not make that mistake. For the sensualist carries his miseries pick-a-back, and round his feet is wound the shroud that shall soon enwrap him. I may be mad, it is true, but I am not so stupid anyhow as to have tried that. No, what is it that makes puppies play with their own tails, that sends cats on their prowling ecstatic errands at night?'

He paused a moment.

'So I went to Nature,' he said. 'I sat down here in this New Forest, sat down fair and square, and looked. That was my first difficulty, to sit here quiet without being bored, to wait without being impatient, to be receptive and very alert, though for a long time nothing particular happened. The change in fact was slow in those early stages.'

'Nothing happened?' asked Darcy, rather impatiently, with the sturdy revolt against any new idea which to the English mind is synonymous with nonsense. 'Why, what in the world *should* happen?'

Now Frank as he had known him was the most generous but most quick-tempered of mortal men; in other words his anger would flare to a prodigious beacon, under almost no provocation, only to be quenched again under a gust of no less impulsive kindliness. Thus the moment Darcy had spoken, an apology for his hasty question was half-way up his tongue. But there was no need for it to have travelled even so far, for Frank laughed again with kindly, genuine mirth.

'Oh, how I should have resented that a few years ago,' he said. 'Thank goodness that resentment is one of the things I have got rid of. I certainly wish that you should believe my story – in fact, you are going to – but that you at this moment should imply that you do not does not concern me.'

'Ah, your solitary sojournings have made you inhuman,' said Darcy, still very English.

'No, human,' said Frank. 'Rather more human, at least rather less of an ape.'

'Well, that was my first quest,' he continued, after a moment, 'the deliberate and unswerving pursuit of joy, and my method, the eager contemplation of Nature. As far as motive went, I dare say it was purely selfish, but as far as effect goes, it seems to me about the best thing one can do for one's fellow-creatures, for happiness is more infectious than small-pox. So, as I said, I sat down and waited; I looked at happy things, zealously avoided the sight of anything unhappy, and by degrees a little trickle of the happiness of this blissful world began to filter into me. The trickle grew more abundant, and now, my dear fellow, if I could for a moment divert from me into you one half of the torrent of joy that pours through me day and night, you would throw the world, art, everything aside, and just live, exist. When a man's body dies, it passes into trees and flowers. Well, that is what I have been trying to do with my soul before death.'

The servant had brought into the pergola a table with syphons and spirits, and had set a lamp upon it. As Frank spoke he leaned forward towards the other, and Darcy for all his matter-of-fact common sense could have sworn that his companion's face shone, was luminous in itself.

His dark brown eyes glowed from within, the unconscious smile of a child irradiated and transformed his face. Darcy felt suddenly excited, exhilarated.

'Go on,' he said. 'Go on. I can feel you are somehow telling me sober truth. I dare say you are mad; but I don't see that matters.'

Frank laughed again.

'Mad?' he said. 'Yes, certainly, if you wish. But I prefer to call it sane. However, nothing matters less than what anybody chooses to call things. God never labels his gifts; He just puts them into our hands; just as he put animals in the garden of Eden, for Adam to name if he felt disposed.'

'So by the continual observance and study of things that were happy,' continued he, 'I got happiness, I got joy. But seeking it, as I did, from Nature, I got much more which I did not seek, but stumbled upon originally by accident. It is difficult to explain, but I will try.

'About three years ago I was sitting one morning in a place I will show you tomorrow. It is down by the river brink, very green, dappled with shade and sun, and the river passes there through some little clumps of reeds. Well, as I sat there, doing nothing, but just looking and listening, I heard the sound quite distinctly of some flute-like instrument playing a strange unending melody. I thought at first it was some musical yokel on the highway and did not pay much attention. But before long the strangeness and indescribable beauty of the tune struck me. It never repeated itself, but it never came to an end, phrase after phrase ran its sweet course, it worked gradually and inevitably up to a climax, and having attained it, it went on; another climax was reached and another and another. Then with a sudden gasp of wonder I localised where it came from. It came from the reeds and from the sky and from the trees. It was everywhere, it was the sound of life. It was, my dear Darcy, as the Greeks would have said, it was Pan playing on his pipes, the voice of Nature. It was the life-melody, the world-melody.'

Darcy was far too interested to interrupt, though there was a question he would have liked to ask, and Frank went on.

'Well, for the moment I was terrified, terrified with the impotent horror of nightmare, and I stopped my ears and just ran from the place and got back to the house panting, trembling, literally in a panic. Unknowingly, for at that time I only pursued joy, I had begun, since I drew my joy from Nature, to get in touch with Nature. Nature, force, God, call it what you will, had drawn across my face a little gossamer web of essential life. I saw that when I emerged from my terror, and I went very humbly back to where I had heard the Pan-pipes. But it was nearly six months before I heard them again.'

'Why was that?' asked Darcy.

'Surely because I had revolted, rebelled, and worst of all been frightened. For I believe that just as there is nothing in the world which so injures one's body as fear, so there is nothing that so much shuts up the soul. I was afraid, you see, of the one thing in the world which has real existence. No wonder its manifestation was withdrawn.'

'And after six months?'

'After six months one blessed morning I heard the piping again. I wasn't afraid that time. And since then it has grown louder, it has become more constant. I now hear it often, and I can put myself into such an attitude towards Nature that the pipes will almost certainly sound. And never yet have they played the same tune, it is always something new, something fuller, richer, more complete than before.'

'What do you mean by "such an attitude towards Nature"?' asked Darcy.

'I can't explain that; but by translating it into a bodily attitude it is this.'

Frank sat up for a moment quite straight in his chair, then slowly sunk back with arms outspread and head drooped.

'That;' he said, 'an effortless attitude, but open, resting, receptive. It is just that which you must do with your soul.'

Then he sat up again.

'One word more,' he said, 'and I will bore you no further. Nor unless you ask me questions shall I talk about it again. You will find me, in fact, quite sane in my mode of life. Birds and beasts you will see behaving somewhat intimately to me, like that moor-hen, but that is all. I will walk with you, ride with you, play golf with you, and talk with you on any subject you like. But I wanted you on the threshold to know what has happened to me. And one thing more will happen.'

He paused again, and a slight look of fear crossed his eyes.

'There will be a final revelation,' he said, 'a complete and blinding stroke which will throw open to me, once and for all, the full knowledge, the full realisation and comprehension that I am one, just as you are, with life. In reality there is no "me", no "you", no "it". Everything is part of the one and only thing which is life. I know that

that is so, but the realisation of it is not yet mine. But it will be, and on that day, so I take it, I shall see Pan. It may mean death, the death of my body, that is, but I don't care. It may mean immortal, eternal life lived here and now and for ever. Then having gained that, ah, my dear Darcy, I shall preach such a gospel of joy, showing myself as the living proof of the truth, that Puritanism, the dismal religion of sour faces, shall vanish like a breath of smoke, and be dispersed and disappear in the sunlit air. But first the full knowledge must be mine.'

Darcy watched his face narrowly.

'You are afraid of that moment,' he said. Frank smiled at him.

'Quite true; you are quick to have seen that. But when it comes I hope I shall not be afraid.'

For some little time there was silence; then Darcy rose.

'You have bewitched me, you extraordinary boy,' he said. 'You have been telling me a fairy-story, and I find myself saying, "Promise me it is true."'

'I promise you that,' said the other.

'And I know I shan't sleep,' added Darcy.

Frank looked at him with a sort of mild wonder as if he scarcely understood.

'Well, what does that matter?' he said.

'I assure you it does. I am wretched unless I sleep.'

'Of course I can make you sleep if I want,' said Frank in a rather bored voice.

'Well, do.'

'Very good: go to bed. I'll come upstairs in ten minutes.'

Frank busied himself for a little after the other had gone, moving the table back under the awning of the verandah and quenching the lamp. Then he went with his quick silent tread upstairs and into Darcy's room. The latter was already in bed, but very wide-eyed and wakeful, and Frank with an amused smile of indulgence, as for a fretful child, sat down on the edge of the bed.

'Look at me,' he said, and Darcy looked.

'The birds are sleeping in the brake,' said Frank softly, 'and the winds are asleep. The sea sleeps, and the tides are but the heaving of its breast. The stars swing slow, rocked in the great cradle of the Heavens, and – '

He stopped suddenly, gently blew out Darcy's candle, and left him sleeping.

Morning brought to Darcy a flood of hard common sense, as clear and crisp as the sunshine that filled his room. Slowly as he woke he gathered together the broken threads of the memories of the evening which had ended, so he told himself, in a trick of common hypnotism. That accounted for it all; the whole strange talk he had had was under a spell of suggestion from the extraordinary vivid boy who had once been a man; all his own excitement, his acceptance of the incredible had been merely the effect of a stronger, more potent will imposed on his own. How strong that will was, he guessed from his own instantaneous obedience to Frank's suggestion of sleep. And armed with impenetrable common sense he came down to breakfast. Frank had already begun, and was consuming a large plateful of porridge and milk with the most prosaic and healthy appetite.

'Slept well?' he asked.

'Yes, of course. Where did you learn hypnotism?'

'By the side of the river.'

'You talked an amazing quantity of nonsense last night,' remarked Darcy, in a voice prickly with reason.

'Rather. I felt quite giddy. Look, I remembered to order a dreadful daily paper for you. You can read about money markets or politics or cricket matches.'

Darcy looked at him closely. In the morning light Frank looked even fresher, younger, more vital than he had done the night before, and the sight of him somehow dinted Darcy's armour of common sense.

'You are the most extraordinary fellow I ever saw,' he said. 'I want to ask you some more questions.'

'Ask away,' said Frank.

For the next day or two Darcy plied his friend with many questions, objections and criticisms on the theory of life, and gradually got out of him a coherent and complete account of his experience. In brief, then, Frank believed that 'by lying naked', as he put it, to the force which controls the passage of the stars, the breaking of a wave, the budding of a tree, the love of a youth and maiden, he had succeeded in a way hitherto undreamed of in possessing himself of the essential principle of life. Day by day, so he thought, he was getting nearer to, and in closer union with, the great power itself which caused all life to be, the spirit of nature, of force, or the spirit of God. For himself, he confessed to what others would call paganism; it was sufficient for him that there existed a principle of life. He did not worship it, he did not pray to it, he did not praise it. Some of it existed in all human beings, just as it existed in trees and animals; to realise and make living to himself the fact that it was all one, was his sole aim and object.

Here perhaps Darcy would put in a word of warning.

'Take care,' he said. 'To see Pan meant death, did it not.'

Frank's eyebrows would rise at this.

'What does that matter?' he said. 'True, the Greeks were always right, and they said so, but there is another possibility. For the nearer I get to it, the more living, the more vital and young I become.'

'What then do you expect the final revelation will do for you?'

'I have told you,' said he. 'It will make me immortal.'

But it was not so much from speech and argument that Darcy grew to grasp his friend's conception, as from the ordinary conduct of his life. They were passing, for instance, one morning down the village street, when an old woman, very bent and decrepit, but with an extraordinary cheerfulness of face, hobbled out from her cottage. Frank instantly stopped when he saw her.

'You old darling! How goes it all?' he said.

But she did not answer, her dim old eyes were riveted on his face; she seemed to drink in like a thirsty creature the beautiful radiance which shone there. Suddenly she put her two withered old hands on his shoulders.

'You're just the sunshine itself,' she said, and he kissed her and passed on.

But scarcely a hundred yards further a strange contradiction of such tenderness occurred. A child running along the path towards them fell on its face and set up a dismal cry of fright and pain. A look of horror came into Frank's eyes, and, putting his fingers in his ears, he fled at full speed down the street, and did not pause till he was out of hearing. Darcy, having ascertained that the child was not really hurt, followed him in bewilderment.

'Are you without pity then?' he asked. Frank shook his head impatiently.

'Can't you see?' he asked. 'Can't you understand that that sort of thing, pain, anger, anything unlovely, throws me back, retards the coming of the great hour! Perhaps when it comes I shall be able to piece that side of life on to the other, on to the true religion of joy. At present I can't.'

'But the old woman. Was she not ugly?'

Frank's radiance gradually returned.

'Ah, no. She was like me. She longed for joy, and knew it when she saw it, the old darling.'

Another question suggested itself.

'Then what about Christianity?' asked Darcy.

'I can't accept it. I can't believe in any creed of which the central doctrine is that God who is Joy should have had to suffer. Perhaps it was so; in some inscrutable way I believe it may have been so, but I don't understand how it was possible. So I leave it alone; my affair is joy.'

They had come to the weir above the village, and the thunder of riotous cool water was heavy in the air. Trees dipped into the translucent stream with slender trailing branches, and the meadow where they stood was starred with midsummer blossomings. Larks shot up carolling into the crystal dome of blue, and a thousand voices of June sang round them. Frank, bare-headed as was his wont, with his coat slung over his arm and his shirt sleeves rolled up above the elbow, stood there like some beautiful wild animal with eyes half-shut and mouth half-open, drinking in the scented warmth of the air. Then suddenly he flung himself face downwards on the grass at the edge of the stream, burying his face in the daisies and cowslips, and lay stretched there in wide-armed ecstasy, with his long fingers pressing and stroking the dewy herbs of the field. Never before had Darcy seen him thus fully possessed by his idea; his caressing fingers, his half-buried face pressed close to the grass, even the clothed lines of his figure were instinct with a vitality that somehow was different from that of other men. And some faint glow from it reached Darcy, some thrill, some vibration from that charged recumbent body passed to him, and for a moment he understood as he had not understood before, despite his persistent questions and the candid answers they received, how real, and how realised by Frank, his idea was.

Then suddenly the muscles in Frank's neck became stiff and alert, and he half-raised his head.

'The Pan-pipes, the Pan-pipes,' he whispered. 'Close, oh, so close.'

Very slowly, as if a sudden movement might interrupt the melody, he raised himself and leaned on the elbow of his bent arm. His eyes opened wider, the lower lids drooped as if he focused his eyes on something very far away, and the smile on his face broadened and quivered like sunlight on still water, till the exultance of its happiness was scarcely human. So he remained motionless and rapt for some minutes, then the look of listening died from his face, and he bowed his head satisfied.

'Ah, that was good,' he said. 'How is it possible you did not hear? Oh, you poor fellow! Did you really hear nothing?'

A week of this outdoor and stimulating life did wonders in restoring to Darcy the vigour and health which his weeks of fever had filched from him, and as his normal activity and higher pressure of vitality returned, he seemed to himself to fall even more under the spell which the miracle of Frank's youth cast over him. Twenty times a day he found himself saying to himself suddenly at the end of some ten minutes' silent resistance to the absurdity of Frank's idea: 'But it isn't possible; it can't be possible,' and from the fact of his having to assure himself so frequently of this, he knew that he was struggling and arguing with a conclusion which already had taken root in his mind. For in any case a visible living miracle confronted him, since it was equally impossible that this youth, this boy, trembling on the verge of manhood, was thirty-five. Yet such was the fact.

July was ushered in by a couple of days of blustering and fretful rain, and Darcy, unwilling to risk a chill, kept to the house. But to Frank this weeping change of weather seemed to have no bearing on the behaviour of man, and he spent his days exactly as he did under the suns of June, lying in his hammock, stretched on the dripping grass, or making huge rambling excursions into the forest, the birds hopping from tree to tree after him, to return in the evening, drenched and soaked, but with the same unquenchable flame of joy burning within him.

'Catch cold?' he would ask; 'I've forgotten how to do it, I think. I suppose it makes one's body more sensible always to sleep out of doors. People who live indoors always remind me of something peeled and skinless.'

'Do you mean to say you slept out-of-doors last night in that deluge?' asked Darcy. 'And where, may I ask?'

Frank thought a moment.

'I slept in the hammock till nearly dawn,' he said. 'For I remember the light blinked in the east when I awoke. Then I went – where did I go – oh, yes, to the meadow where the Pan-pipes sounded so close a week ago. You were with me, do you remember? But I always have a rug if it is wet.'

And he went whistling upstairs.

Somehow that little touch, his obvious effort to recall where he had slept, brought strangely home to Darcy the wonderful romance of which he was the still half-incredulous beholder. Sleep till close on dawn in a hammock, then the tramp – or probably scamper – underneath the windy and weeping heavens to the remote and lonely meadow by the weir! The picture of other such nights rose before him; Frank sleeping perhaps by the bathing-place under the filtered twilight of the stars, or the white blaze of moonshine, a stir and awakening at some dead hour, perhaps a space of silent wide-eyed thought, and then a-wandering through the hushed woods to some other dormitory, alone with his happiness, alone with the joy and the life that suffused and enveloped him, without other thought or desire or aim except the hourly and never-ceasing communion with the joy of nature.

They were in the middle of dinner that night, talking on indifferent subjects, when Darcy suddenly broke off in the middle of a sentence.

'I've got it,' he said. 'At last I've got it.'

'Congratulate you,' said Frank. 'But what?'

'The radical unsoundness of your idea. It is this: "All Nature from highest to lowest is full, crammed full of suffering; every living organism in Nature preys on another, yet in your aim to get close to, to be one with Nature, you leave suffering altogether out; you run away from it, you refuse to recognise it. And you are waiting, you say, for the final revelation." '

Frank's brow clouded slightly.

'Well,' he asked, rather wearily.

'Cannot you guess then when the final revelation will be? In joy you are supreme, I grant you that; I did not know a man could be so master of it. You have learned perhaps practically all that Nature can teach. And if, as you think, the final revelation is coming to you, it will be the revelation of horror, suffering, death, pain in all its hideous forms. Suffering does exist: you hate it and fear it.'

Frank held up his hand.

'Stop; let me think,' he said.

There was silence for a long minute.

'That never struck me,' he said at length. 'It is possible that what you suggest is true. Does the sight of Pan mean that, do you think? Is it that Nature, take it altogether, suffers horribly, suffers to a hideous inconceivable extent? Shall I be shown all the suffering?'

He got up and came round to where Darcy sat.

'If it is so, so be it,' he said. 'Because, my dear fellow, I am near, so splendidly near to the final revelation. Today the pipes have sounded almost without pause. I have even heard the rustle in the bushes, I believe, of Pan's coming. I have seen, yes, I saw today, the bushes pushed aside as if by a hand, and piece of a face, not human, peered through. But I was not frightened, at least I did not run away this time.'

He took a turn up to the window and back again.

'Yes, there is suffering all through,' he said, 'and I have left it all out of my search. Perhaps, as you say, the revelation will be that. And in that case, it will be goodbye. I have gone on one line. I shall have gone too far along one road, without having explored the other. But I can't go back now. I wouldn't if I could; not a step would I retrace! In any case, whatever the revelation is, it will be God. I'm sure of that.'

The rainy weather soon passed, and with the return of the sun Darcy again joined Frank in long rambling days. It grew extraordinarily hotter, and with the fresh bursting of life, after the rain, Frank's vitality seemed to blaze higher and higher. Then, as is the habit of the English weather, one evening clouds began to bank themselves up in the west, the sun went down in a glare of coppery thunder-rack, and the whole earth broiling under an unspeakable oppression and sultriness paused and panted for the storm. After sunset the remote fires of lightning began to wink and flicker on the horizon, but when bed-time came the storm seemed to have moved no nearer, though a very low unceasing noise of thunder was audible. Weary and oppressed by the stress of the day, Darcy fell at once into a heavy uncomforting sleep.

He woke suddenly into full consciousness, with the din of some appalling explosion of thunder in his ears, and sat up in bed with racing heart. Then for a moment, as he recovered himself from the panic-land which lies between sleeping and waking, there was silence, except for the steady hissing of rain on the shrubs outside his window. But suddenly that silence was shattered and shredded into fragments by a scream from somewhere close at hand outside in the black garden, a scream of supreme and despairing terror. Again and once again it shrilled up, and then a babble of awful words was interjected. A quivering sobbing voice that he knew said: 'My God, oh, my God; oh, Christ!'

And then followed a little mocking, bleating laugh. Then was silence again; only the rain hissed on the shrubs.

All this was but the affair of a moment, and without pause either to put on clothes or light a candle, Darcy was already fumbling at his door-handle. Even as he opened it he met a terror-stricken face outside, that of the man-servant who carried a light.

'Did you hear?' he asked.

The man's face was bleached to a dull shining whiteness.

'Yes, sir,' he said. 'It was the master's voice.'

Together they hurried down the stairs and through the dining-room where an orderly table for breakfast had already been laid, and out on to the terrace. The rain for the moment had been utterly stayed, as if the tap of the heavens had been turned off, and under the lowering black sky, not quite dark, since the moon rode somewhere serene behind the conglomerated thunder-clouds, Darcy stumbled into the garden, followed by the servant with the candle. The monstrous leaping shadow of himself was cast before him on the lawn; lost and wandering odours of rose and lily and damp earth were thick about him, but more pungent was some sharp and acrid smell that suddenly reminded him of a certain châlet in which he had once taken refuge in the Alps. In the blackness of the hazy light from the sky, and the vague tossing of the candle behind him, he saw that the hammock in which Frank so often lay was tenanted. A gleam of white shirt was there, as if a man were sitting up in it, but across that there was an obscure dark shadow, and as he approached the acrid odour grew more intense.

He was now only some few yards away, when suddenly the black shadow seemed to jump into the air, then came down with tappings of hard hoofs on the brick path that ran down the pergola, and with frolicsome skippings galloped off into the bushes. When that was gone Darcy could see quite clearly that a shirted figure sat up in the hammock. For one moment, from sheer terror of the unseen, he hung on his step, and the servant joining him they walked together to the hammock.

It was Frank. He was in shirt and trousers only, and he sat up with braced arms. For one half-second he stared at them, his face a mask of horrible contorted terror. His upper lip was drawn back so that the gums of the teeth appeared, and his eyes were focused not on the two who approached him, but on something quite close to him; his nostrils were widely expanded, as if he panted for breath, and terror incarnate and repulsion and deathly anguish ruled dreadful lines on his smooth cheeks and forehead. Then even as they looked the body sank backwards, and the ropes of the hammock wheezed and strained.

Darcy lifted him out and carried him indoors. Once he thought there was a faint convulsive stir of the limbs that lay with so dead a weight in his arms, but when they got inside, there was no trace of life. But the look of supreme terror and agony of fear had gone from his face, a boy tired with play but still smiling in his sleep was the burden he laid on the floor. His eyes had closed, and the beautiful mouth lay in smiling curves, even as when a few mornings ago, in the meadow by the weir, it had quivered to the music of the unheard melody of Pan's pipes. Then they looked further.

*

Frank had come back from his bathe before dinner that night in his usual costume of shirt and trousers only. He had not dressed, and during dinner, so Darcy remembered, he had rolled up the sleeves of his shirt to above the elbow. Later, as they sat and talked after dinner on the close sultriness of the evening, he had unbuttoned the front of his shirt to let what little breath of wind there was play on his skin. The sleeves were rolled up now, the front of the shirt was unbuttoned, and on his arms and on the brown skin of his chest were strange discolorations which grew momently more clear and defined, till they saw that the marks were pointed prints, as if caused by the hoofs of some monstrous goat that had leaped and stamped upon him.

Mrs Amworth

The village of Maxley, where, last summer and autumn, these strange events took place, lies on a heathery and pine-clad upland of Sussex. In all England you could not find a sweeter and saner situation. Should the wind blow from the south, it comes laden with the spices of the sea; to the east high downs protect it from the inclemencies of March; and from the west and north the breezes which reach it travel over miles of aromatic forest and heather. The village itself is insignificant enough in point of population, but rich in amenities and beauty. Half-way down the single street, with its broad road and spacious areas of grass on each side, stands the little Norman Church and the antique graveyard long disused: for the rest there are a dozen small, sedate Georgian houses, red-bricked and long-windowed, each with a square of flower-garden in front, and an ampler strip behind; a score of shops, and a couple of score of thatched cottages belonging to labourers on neighbouring estates, complete the entire cluster of its peaceful habitations. The general peace, however, is sadly broken on Saturdays and Sundays, for we lie on one of the main roads between London and Brighton and our quiet street becomes a racecourse for flying motor-cars and bicycles.

A notice just outside the village begging them to go slowly only seems to encourage them to accelerate their speed, for the road lies open and straight, and there is really no reason why they should do otherwise. By way of protest, therefore, the ladies of Maxley cover their noses and mouths with their handkerchiefs as they see a motor-car approaching, though, as the street is asphalted, they need not really take these precautions against dust. But late on Sunday night the horde of scorchers has passed, and we settle down again to five days of cheerful and leisurely seclusion. Railway strikes which agitate the country so much leave us undisturbed because most of the inhabitants of Maxley never leave it at all.

I am the fortunate possessor of one of these small Georgian houses, and consider myself no less fortunate in having so interesting and stimulating a neighbour as Francis Urcombe, who, the most confirmed of Maxleyites, has not slept away from his house, which stands just opposite to mine in the village street, for nearly two years, at which date, though still in middle life, he resigned his Physiological Professorship at Cambridge University and devoted himself to the study of those occult and curious phenomena which seem equally to concern the physical and the psychical sides of human nature. Indeed his retirement was not unconnected with his passion for the strange uncharted places that lie on the confines and borders of science, the existence of which is so stoutly denied by the more materialistic minds, for he advocated that all medical students should be obliged to pass some sort of examination in mesmerism, and that one of the tripos papers should be designed to test their knowledge in such subjects as appearances at time of death, haunted houses, vampirism, automatic writing, and possession.

'Of course they wouldn't listen to me,' ran his account of the matter, 'for there is nothing that these seats of learning are so frightened of as knowledge, and the road to knowledge lies in the study of things like these. The functions of the human frame are, broadly speaking, known. They are a country, anyhow, that has been charted and mapped out. But outside that lie huge tracts of undiscovered country, which certainly exist, and the real pioneers of knowledge are those who, at the cost of being derided as credulous and superstitious, want to push on into those misty and probably perilous places. I felt that I could be of more use by setting out without compass or knapsack into the mists than by sitting in a cage like a canary and chirping about what was known. Besides, teaching is very bad for a man who knows himself only to be a learner: you only need to be a self-conceited ass to teach.'

Here, then, in Francis Urcombe, was a delightful neighbour to one who, like myself, has an uneasy and burning curiosity about what he called the 'misty and perilous places'; and this last spring we had a further and most welcome addition to our pleasant little community, in the person of Mrs Amworth, widow of an Indian civil servant. Her husband had been a judge in the North-West Provinces, and after his death at Peshawar she came back to England, and after a year in London found herself starving for the ampler air and sunshine of the country to take the place of the fogs and griminess of town. She had, too, a special reason for settling in Maxley, since her ancestors up till a hundred years ago had long been native to the place, and in the old churchyard, now disused, are many gravestones bearing her maiden name of Chaston. Big and energetic, her vigorous and genial personality speedily woke Maxley up to a higher degree of sociality than it had ever known. Most of us were bachelors or spinsters or elderly folk not much inclined to exert ourselves in the expense and effort of hospitality, and hitherto the gaiety of a small tea-party, with bridge afterwards and goloshes (when it was wet) to trip home in again for a solitary dinner, was about the climax of our festivities. But Mrs Amworth showed us a more gregarious way, and set an example of luncheon-parties and little dinners, which we began to follow. On other nights when no such hospitality was on foot, a lone man like myself found it pleasant to know that a call on the telephone to Mrs Amworth's house not a hundred yards off, and an inquiry as to whether I might come over after dinner for a game of piquet before bed-time, would probably evoke a response of welcome. There she would be, with a comrade-like eagerness for companionship, and there was a glass of port and a cup of coffee and a cigarette and a game of piquet. She played the piano, too, in a free and exuberant manner, and had a charming voice and sang to her own accompaniment; and as the days grew long and the light lingered late, we played our game in her garden, which in the course of a few months she had turned from being a nursery for slugs and snails into a glowing patch of luxuriant blossoming. She was always cheery and jolly; she was interested in everything, and in music, in gardening, in games of all sorts was a competent performer. Everybody (with one exception) liked her, everybody felt her to bring with her the tonic of a sunny day. That one exception was Francis Urcombe; he, though he confessed he did not like her, acknowledged that he was vastly interested in her. This always seemed strange to me, for pleasant and jovial as she was, I could see nothing in her that could call forth conjecture or intrigued surmise, so healthy and unmysterious a figure did she present. But of the genuineness of Urcombe's interest there could be no doubt; one could see him watching and scrutinising her. In matter of age, she frankly volunteered the information that she was forty-five; but her briskness, her activity, her unravaged skin, her coal-black hair, made it difficult to believe that she was not adopting an unusual device, and adding ten years on to her age instead of subtracting them.

Often, also, as our quite unsentimental friendship ripened, Mrs Amworth would ring me up and propose her advent. If I was busy writing, I was to give her, so we definitely bargained, a frank negative, and in answer I could hear her jolly laugh and her wishes for a successful evening of work. Sometimes, before her proposal arrived, Urcombe would already have stepped across from his house opposite for a smoke and a chat, and he, hearing who my intending visitor was, always urged me to beg her to come. She and I should play our piquet, said he, and he would look on, if we did not object, and learn something of the game. But I doubt whether he paid much attention to it, for nothing could be clearer than that, under that penthouse of forehead and thick eyebrows, his attention was fixed not on the cards, but on one of the players. But he seemed to enjoy an hour spent thus, and often, until one particular evening in July, he would watch her with the air of a man who has some deep problem in front of him. She, enthusiastically keen about our game, seemed not to notice his scrutiny. Then came that evening, when, as I see in the light of subsequent events, began the first twitching of the veil that hid the secret horror from my eyes. I did not know it then, though I noticed that thereafter, if she rang up to propose coming round, she always asked not only if I was at leisure, but whether Mr Urcombe was with me. If so, she said, she would not spoil the chat of two old bachelors, and laughingly wished me good night.

Urcombe, on this occasion, had been with me for some half-hour before Mrs Amworth's appearance, and had been talking to me about the mediaeval beliefs concerning vampirism, one of those borderland subjects which he declared had not been sufficiently studied before it had been consigned by the medical profession to the dust-heap of exploded superstitions. There he sat, grim and eager, tracing, with that pellucid clearness which had made him in his Cambridge days so admirable a lecturer, the history of those mysterious visitations. In them all there were the same general features: one of those ghoulish spirits took up its abode in a living man or woman, conferring supernatural powers of bat-like flight and glutting itself with nocturnal blood-feasts. When its host died it continued to dwell in the corpse, which remained undecayed. By day it rested, by night it left the grave and went on its awful errands. No European country in the Middle Ages seemed to have escaped them; earlier yet, parallels were to be found, in Roman and Greek and in Jewish history.

'It's a large order to set all that evidence aside as being moonshine,' he said. 'Hundreds of totally independent witnesses in many ages have testified to the occurrence of these phenomena, and there's no explanation known to me which covers all the facts. And if you feel inclined to say "Why, then, if these are facts, do we not come across them now?" there are two answers I can make you. One is that there were diseases known in the Middle Ages, such as the black death; which were certainly existent then and which have become extinct since, but for that reason we do not assert that such diseases never existed. Just as the black death visited England and decimated the population of Norfolk, so here in this very district about three hundred years ago there was certainly an outbreak of vampirism, and Maxley was the centre of it. My second answer is even more convincing, for I tell you that vampirism is by no means extinct now. An outbreak of it certainly occurred in India a year or two ago.'

At that moment I heard my knocker plied in the cheerful and peremptory manner in which Mrs Amworth is accustomed to announce her arrival, and I went to the door to open it.

'Come in at once,' I said, 'and save me from having my blood curdled. Mr Urcombe has been trying to alarm me.'

Instantly her vital, voluminous presence seemed to fill the room.

'Ah, but how lovely!' she said. 'I delight in having my blood curdled. Go on with your ghost-story, Mr Urcombe. I adore ghost-stories.'

I saw that, as his habit was, he was intently observing her.

'It wasn't a ghost-story exactly,' said he. 'I was only telling our host how vampirism was not extinct yet. I was saying that there was an outbreak of it in India only a few years ago.'

There was a more than perceptible pause, and I saw that, if Urcombe was observing her, she on her side was observing him with fixed eye and parted mouth. Then her jolly laugh invaded that rather tense silence.

'Oh, what a shame!' she said. 'You're not going to curdle my blood at all. Where did you pick up such a tale, Mr Urcombe? I have lived for years in India and never heard a rumour of such a thing. Some story-teller in the bazaars must have invented it: they are famous at that.'

I could see that Urcombe was on the point of saying something further, but checked himself.

'Ah! very likely that was it,' he said.

But something had disturbed our usual peaceful sociability that night, and something had damped Mrs Amworth's usual high spirits. She had no gusto for her piquet, and left after a couple of games. Urcombe had been silent too, indeed he hardly spoke again till she departed.

'That was unfortunate,' he said, 'for the outbreak of – of a very mysterious disease, let us call it, took place at Peshawar, where she and her husband were. And – '

'Well?' I asked.

'He was one of the victims of it,' said he. 'Naturally I had quite forgotten that when I spoke.'

The summer was unreasonably hot and rainless, and Maxley suffered much from drought, and also from a plague of big black night-flying gnats, the bite of which was very irritating and virulent. They came sailing in of an evening, settling on one's skin so quietly that one perceived nothing till the sharp stab announced that one had been bitten. They did not bite the hands or face, but chose always the neck and throat for their feeding-ground, and most of us, as the poison spread, assumed a temporary goitre. Then about the middle of August appeared the first of those mysterious cases of illness which our local doctor attributed to the long-continued heat coupled with the bite of these venomous insects. The patient was a boy of sixteen or seventeen, the son of Mrs Amworth's gardener, and the symptoms were an anaemic pallor and a languid prostration, accompanied by great drowsiness and an abnormal appetite. He had, too, on his throat two small punctures where, so Dr Ross conjectured, one of these great gnats had bitten him. But the odd thing was that there was no swelling or inflammation round the place where he had been bitten. The heat at this time had begun to abate, but the cooler weather failed to restore him, and the boy, in spite of the quantity of good food which he so ravenously swallowed, wasted away to a skin-clad skeleton.

I met Dr Ross in the street one afternoon about this time, and in answer to my inquiries about his patient he said that he was afraid the boy was dying. The case, he confessed, completely puzzled him: some obscure form of pernicious anaemia was all he could suggest. But he wondered whether Mr Urcombe would consent to see the boy, on the chance of his being able to throw some new light on the case, and since Urcombe was dining with me that night, I proposed to Dr Ross to join us. He could not do this, but said he would look in later. When he came, Urcombe at once consented to put his skill at the other's disposal, and together they went off at once. Being thus shorn of my sociable evening, I telephoned to Mrs Amworth to know if I might inflict myself on her for an hour. Her answer was a welcoming affirmative, and between piquet and music the hour lengthened itself into two. She spoke of the boy who was lying so desperately and mysteriously ill, and told me that she had often been to see him, taking him nourishing and delicate food. But today – and her kind eyes moistened as she spoke – she was afraid she had paid her last visit. Knowing the antipathy between her and Urcombe, I did not tell her that he had been called into consultation; and when I returned home she accompanied me to my door, for the sake of a breath of night air, and in order to borrow a magazine which contained an article on gardening which she wished to read.

'Ah, this delicious night air,' she said, luxuriously sniffing in the coolness. 'Night air and gardening are the great tonics. There is nothing so stimulating as bare contact with rich mother earth. You are never so fresh as when you have been grubbing in the soil – black hands, black nails, and boots covered with mud.' She gave her great jovial laugh.

'I'm a glutton for air and earth,' she said. 'Positively I look forward to death, for then I shall be buried and have the kind earth all round me. No leaden caskets for me – I have given explicit directions. But what shall I do about air? Well, I suppose one can't have everything. The magazine? A thousand thanks, I will faithfully return it. Good night: garden and keep your windows open, and you won't have anaemia.'

'I always sleep with my windows open,' said I.

I went straight up to my bedroom, of which one of the windows looks out over the street, and as I undressed I thought I heard voices talking outside not far away. But I paid no particular attention, put out my lights, and falling asleep plunged into the depths of a most horrible dream, distortedly suggested no doubt, by my last words with Mrs Amworth. I dreamed that I woke, and found that both my bedroom windows were shut. Half-suffocating I dreamed that I sprang out of bed, and went across to open them. The blind over the first was drawn down, and pulling it up I saw, with the indescribable horror of incipient nightmare, Mrs Amworth's face suspended close to the pane in the darkness outside, nodding and smiling at me. Pulling down the blind again to keep that terror out, I rushed to the second window on the other side of the room, and there again was Mrs Amworth's face. Then the panic came upon me in full blast; here was I suffocating in the airless room, and whichever window I opened Mrs Amworth's face would float in, like those noiseless black gnats that bit before one was aware. The nightmare rose to screaming point, and with strangled yells I awoke to find my room cool and quiet with both windows open and blinds up and a half-moon high in its course, casting an oblong of tranquil light on the floor. But even when I was awake the horror persisted, and I lay tossing and turning. I must have slept long before the nightmare seized me, for now it was nearly day, and soon in the east the drowsy eyelids of morning began to lift.

I was scarcely downstairs next morning – for after the dawn I slept late – when Urcombe rang up to know if he might see me immediately. He came in, grim and preoccupied, and I noticed that he was pulling on a pipe that was not even filled.

'I want your help,' he said, 'and so I must tell you first of all what happened last night. I went round with the little doctor to see his patient, and found him just alive, but scarcely more. I instantly diagnosed in my own mind what this anaemia, unaccountable by any other explanation, meant. The boy is the prey of a vampire.'

He put his empty pipe on the breakfast-table, by which I had just sat down, and folded his arms, looking at me steadily from under his overhanging brows.

'Now about last night,' he said. 'I insisted that he should be moved from his father's cottage into my house. As we were carrying him on a stretcher, whom should we meet but Mrs Amworth? She expressed shocked surprise that we were moving him. Now why do you think she did that?'

With a start of horror, as I remembered my dream that night before, I felt an idea come into my mind so preposterous and unthinkable that I instantly turned it out again.

'I haven't the smallest idea,' I said.

'Then listen, while I tell you about what happened later. I put out all light in the room where the boy lay, and watched. One window was a little open, for I had forgotten to close it, and about midnight I heard something outside, trying apparently to push it farther open. I guessed who it was – yes, it was full twenty feet from the ground – and I peeped round the corner of the blind. Just outside was the face of Mrs Amworth and her hand was on the frame of the window. Very softly I crept close, and then banged the window down, and I think I just caught the tip of one of her fingers.'

'But it's impossible,' I cried. 'How could she be floating in the air like that? And what had she come for? Don't tell me such – '

Once more, with closer grip, the remembrance of my nightmare seized me.

'I am telling you what I saw,' said he. 'And all night long, until it was nearly day, she was fluttering outside, like some terrible bat, trying to gain admittance. Now put together various things I have told you.'

He began checking them off on his fingers.

'Number one,' he said: 'there was an outbreak of disease similar to that which this boy is suffering from at Peshawar, and her husband died of it. Number two: Mrs Amworth protested against my moving the boy to my house. Number three: she, or the demon that inhabits her body, a creature powerful and deadly, tries to gain admittance. And add this, too: in mediaeval times there was an epidemic of vampirism here at Maxley. The vampire, so the accounts run, was found to be Elizabeth Chaston . . . I see you remember Mrs Amworth's maiden name. Finally, the boy is stronger this morning. He would certainly not have been alive if he had been visited again. And what do you make of it?'

There was a long silence, during which I found this incredible horror assuming the hues of reality.

'I have something to add,' I said, 'which may or may not bear on it. You say that the – the spectre went away shortly before dawn.'

'Yes.'

I told him of my dream, and he smiled grimly.

'Yes, you did well to awake,' he said. 'That warning came from your subconscious self, which never wholly slumbers, and cried out to you of deadly danger. For two reasons, then, you must help me: one to save others, the second to save yourself.'

'What do you want me to do?' I asked.

'I want you first of all to help me in watching this boy, and ensuring that she does not come near him. Eventually I want you to help me in tracking the thing down, in exposing and destroying it. It is not human: it is an incarnate fiend. What steps we shall have to take I don't yet know.'

It was now eleven of the forenoon, and presently I went across to his house for a twelve-hour vigil while he slept, to come on duty again that night, so that for the next twenty-four hours either Urcombe or myself was always in the room where the boy, now getting stronger every hour, was lying. The day following was Saturday and a morning of brilliant, pellucid weather, and already when I went across to his house to resume my duty the stream of motors down to Brighton had begun. Simultaneously I saw Urcombe with a cheerful face, which boded good news of his patient, coming out of his house, and Mrs Amworth, with a gesture of salutation to me and a basket in her hand, walking up the broad strip of grass which bordered the road. There we all three met. I noticed (and saw that Urcombe noticed it too) that one finger of her left hand was bandaged.

'Good morning to you both,' said she. 'And I hear your patient is doing well, Mr Urcombe. I have come to bring him a bowl of jelly, and to sit with him for an hour. He and I are great friends. I am overjoyed at his recovery.'

Urcombe paused a moment, as if making up his mind, and then shot out a pointing finger at her.

'I forbid that,' he said. 'You shall not sit with him or see him. And you know the reason as well as I do.'

I have never seen so horrible a change pass over a human face as that which now blanched hers to the colour of a grey mist. She put up her hand as if to shield herself from that pointing finger, which drew the sign of the cross in the air, and shrank back cowering on to the road. There was a wild hoot from a horn, a grinding of brakes, a shout – too late – from a passing car, and one long scream suddenly cut short. Her body rebounded from the roadway after the first wheel had gone over it, and the second followed. It lay there, quivering and twitching, and was still.

She was buried three days afterwards in the cemetery outside Maxley, in accordance with the wishes she had told me that she had devised about her interment, and the shock which her sudden and awful death had caused to the little community began by degrees to pass off. To two people only, Urcombe and myself, the horror of it was mitigated from the first by the nature of the relief that her death brought; but, naturally enough, we kept our own counsel, and no hint of what greater horror had been thus averted was ever let slip. But, oddly enough, so it seemed to me, he was still not satisfied about something in connection with her, and would give no answer to my questions on the subject. Then as the days of a tranquil mellow September and the October that followed began to drop away like the leaves of the yellowing trees, his uneasiness relaxed. But before the entry of November the seeming tranquillity broke into hurricane.

I had been dining one night at the far end of the village, and about eleven o'clock was walking home again. The moon was of an unusual brilliance, rendering all that it shone on as distinct as in some etching. I had just come opposite the house which Mrs Amworth had occupied, where there was a board up telling that it was to let, when

I heard the click of her front gate, and next moment I saw, with a sudden chill and quaking of my very spirit, that she stood there. Her profile, vividly illuminated, was turned to me, and I could not be mistaken in my identification of her. She appeared not to see me (indeed the shadow of the yew hedge in front of her garden enveloped me in its blackness) and she went swiftly across the road, and entered the gate of the house directly opposite. There I lost sight of her completely.

My breath was coming in short pants as if I had been running – and now indeed I ran, with fearful backward glances, along the hundred yards that separated me from my house and Urcombe's. It was to his that my flying steps took me, and next minute I was within.

'What have you come to tell me?' he asked. 'Or shall I guess?'

'You can't guess,' said I.

'No; it's no guess. She has come back and you have seen her. Tell me about it.'

I gave him my story.

'That's Major Pearsall's house,' he said. 'Come back with me there at once.'

'But what can we do?' I asked.

'I've no idea. That's what we have got to find out.'

A minute later, we were opposite the house. When I had passed it before, it was all dark; now lights gleamed from a couple of windows upstairs. Even as we faced it, the front door opened, and next moment Major Pearsall emerged from the gate. He saw us and stopped.

'I'm on my way to Dr Ross,' he said quickly, 'My wife has been taken suddenly ill. She had been in bed an hour when I came upstairs, and I found her white as a ghost and utterly exhausted. She had been to sleep, it seemed – but you will excuse me.'

'One moment, Major,' said Urcombe. 'Was there any mark on her throat?'

'How did you guess that?' said he. 'There was: one of those beastly gnats must have bitten her twice there. She was streaming with blood.'

'And there's someone with her?' asked Urcombe.

'Yes, I roused her maid.'

He went off, and Urcombe turned to me. 'I know now what we have to do,' he said. 'Change your clothes, and I'll join you at your house.'

'What is it?' I asked.

'I'll tell you on our way. We're going to the cemetery.'

He carried a pick, a shovel, and a screwdriver when he rejoined me, and wore round his shoulders a long coil of rope. As we walked, he gave me the outlines of the ghastly hour that lay before us.

'What I have to tell you,' he said, 'will seem to you now too fantastic for credence, but before dawn we shall see whether it outstrips reality. By a most fortunate happening, you saw the spectre, the astral body, whatever you choose to call it, of Mrs Amworth, going on its grisly business, and therefore, beyond doubt, the vampire spirit which abode in her during life animates her again in death. That is not exceptional – indeed, all these weeks since her death I have been expecting it. If I am right, we shall find her body undecayed and untouched by corruption.'

'But she has been dead nearly two months,' said I.

'If she had been dead two years it would still be so, if the vampire has possession of her. So remember: whatever you see done, it will be done not to her, who in the natural course would now be feeding the grasses above her grave, but to a spirit of untold evil and malignancy, which gives a phantom life to her body.'

'But what shall I see done?' said I.

'I will tell you. We know that now, at this moment, the vampire clad in her mortal semblance is out; dining out. But it must get back before dawn, and it will pass into the material form that lies in her grave. We must wait for that, and then with your help I shall dig up her body. If I am right, you will look on her as she was in life, with the full vigour of the dreadful nutriment she has received pulsing in her veins. And then, when dawn has come, and the vampire cannot leave the lair of her body, I shall strike her with this' – and he pointed to his pick – 'through the heart, and she, who comes to life again only with the animation the fiend gives her, she and her hellish partner will be dead indeed. Then we must bury her again, delivered at last.'

We had come to the cemetery, and in the brightness of the moonshine there was no difficulty in identifying her grave. It lay some twenty yards from the small chapel, in the porch of which, obscured by shadow, we concealed ourselves. From there we had a clear and open sight of the grave, and now we must wait till its infernal visitor returned home. The night was warm and windless, yet even if a freezing wind had been raging I think I should have felt nothing of it, so intense was my preoccupation as to what the night and dawn would bring. There was a bell in the turret of the chapel, that struck the quarters of the hour, and it amazed me to find how swiftly the chimes succeeded one another.

The moon had long set, but a twilight of stars shone in a clear sky, when five o'clock of the morning sounded from the turret. A few minutes more passed, and then I felt Urcombe's hand softly nudging me; and looking out in the direction of his pointing finger, I saw that the form of a woman, tall and large in build, was approaching from the right. Noiselessly, with a motion more of gliding and floating than walking, she moved across the cemetery to the grave which was the centre of our observation. She moved round it as if to be certain of its identity, and for a moment stood directly facing us. In the greyness to which now my eyes had grown accustomed, I could easily see her face, and recognise its features.

She drew her hand across her mouth as if wiping it, and broke into a chuckle of such laughter as made my hair stir on my head. Then she leaped on to the grave, holding her hands high above her head, and inch by inch disappeared into the earth. Urcombe's hand was laid on my arm, in an injunction to keep still, but now he removed it.

'Come,' he said.

With pick and shovel and rope we went to the grave. The earth was light and sandy, and soon after six struck we had delved down to the coffin lid. With his pick he loosened the earth round it, and, adjusting the rope through the handles by which it had been lowered, we tried to raise it. This was a long and laborious business, and the light had begun to herald day in the east before we had it out, and lying by the side of the grave. With his screwdriver he loosed the fastenings of the lid, and slid it aside, and standing there we looked on the face of Mrs Amworth. The eyes, once closed in death, were open, the cheeks were flushed with colour, the red, full-lipped mouth seemed to smile.

'One blow and it is all over,' he said. 'You need not look.'

Even as he spoke he took up the pick again, and, laying the point of it on her left breast, measured his distance. And though I knew what was coming I could not look away . . .

He grasped the pick in both hands, raised it an inch or two for the taking of his aim, and then with full force brought it down on her breast. A fountain of blood, though she had been dead so long, spouted high in the air, falling with the thud of a heavy splash over the shroud, and simultaneously from those red lips came one long, appalling cry, swelling up like some hooting siren, and dying away again. With that, instantaneous as a lightning flash, came the touch of corruption on her face, the colour of it faded to ash, the plump cheeks fell in, the mouth dropped.

'Thank God, that's over,' said he, and without pause slipped the coffin lid back into its place.

Day was coming fast now, and, working like men possessed, we lowered the coffin into its place again, and shovelled the earth over it . . . . The birds were busy with their earliest pipings as we went back to Maxley.

The Room in the Tower

It is probable that everybody who is at all a constant dreamer has had at least one experience of an event or a sequence of circumstances which have come to his mind in sleep being subsequently realised in the material world. But, in my opinion, so far from this being a strange thing, it would be far odder if this fulfilment did not occasionally happen, since our dreams are, as a rule, concerned with people whom we know and places with which we are familiar, such as might very naturally occur in the awake and daylit world. True, these dreams are often broken into by some absurd and fantastic incident, which puts them out of court in regard to their subsequent fulfilment, but on the mere calculation of chances, it does not appear in the least unlikely that a dream imagined by anyone who dreams constantly should occasionally come true. Not long ago, for instance, I experienced such a fulfilment of a dream which seems to me in no way remarkable and to have no kind of psychical significance. The manner of it was as follows.

A certain friend of mine, living abroad, is amiable enough to write to me about once in a fortnight. Thus, when fourteen days or thereabouts have elapsed since I last heard from him, my mind, probably, either consciously or subconsciously, is expectant of a letter from him. One night last week I dreamed that as I was going upstairs to dress for dinner I heard, as I often heard, the sound of the postman's knock on my front door, and diverted my direction downstairs instead. There, among other correspondence, was a letter from him. Thereafter the fantastic entered, for on opening it I found inside the ace of diamonds, and scribbled across it in his well-known handwriting, 'I am sending you this for safe custody, as you know it is running an unreasonable risk to keep aces in Italy.' The next evening I was just preparing to go upstairs to dress when I heard the post-man's knock, and did precisely as I had done in my dream. There, among other letters, was one from my friend. Only it did not contain the ace of diamonds. Had it done so, I should have attached more weight to the matter, which, as it stands, seems to me a perfectly ordinary coincidence. No doubt I consciously or subconsciously expected a letter from him, and this suggested to me my dream. Similarly, the fact that my friend had not written to me for a fortnight suggested to him that he should do so. But occasionally it is not so easy to find such an explanation, and for the following story I can find no explanation at all. It came out of the dark, and into the dark it has gone again.

All my life I have been a habitual dreamer: the nights are few, that is to say, when I do not find on awaking in the morning that some mental experience has been mine, and sometimes, all night long, apparently, a series of the most dazzling adventures befall me. Almost without exception these adventures are pleasant, though often merely trivial. It is of an exception that I am going to speak.

It was when I was about sixteen that a certain dream first came to me, and this is how it befell. It opened with my being set down at the door of a big red-brick house, where, I understood, I was going to stay. The servant who opened the door told me that tea was being served in the garden, and led me through a low dark-panelled hall, with a large open fireplace, on to a cheerful green lawn set round with flower beds. There were grouped about the tea-table a small party of people, but they were all strangers to me except one, who was a schoolfellow called Jack Stone, clearly the son of the house, and he introduced me to his mother and father and a couple of sisters. I was, I remember, somewhat astonished to find myself here, for the boy in question was scarcely known to me, and I rather disliked what I knew of him; moreover, he had left school nearly a year before. The afternoon was very hot, and an intolerable oppression reigned. On the far side of the lawn ran a red-brick wall, with an iron gate in its centre, outside which stood a walnut tree. We sat in the shadow of the house opposite a row of long windows, inside which I could see a table with cloth laid, glimmering with glass and silver. This garden front of the house was very long, and at one end of it stood a tower of three storeys, which looked to me much older than the rest of the building.

Before long, Mrs Stone, who, like the rest of the party, had sat in absolute silence, said to me, 'Jack will show you your room: I have given you the room in the tower.'

Quite inexplicably my heart sank at her words. I felt as if I had known that I should have the room in the tower, and that it contained something dreadful and significant. Jack instantly got up, and I understood that I had to follow him. In silence we passed through the hall, and mounted a great oak staircase with many corners, and arrived at a small landing with two doors set in it. He pushed one of these open for me to enter, and without coming in himself, closed it after me. Then I knew that my conjecture had been right: there was something awful in the room, and with the terror of nightmare growing swiftly and enveloping me, I awoke in a spasm of terror.

Now that dream or variations on it occurred to me intermittently for fifteen years. Most often it came in exactly this form, the arrival, the tea laid out on the lawn, the deadly silence succeeded by that one deadly sentence, the mounting with Jack Stone up to the room in the tower where horror dwelt, and it always came to a close in the nightmare of terror at that which was in the room, though I never saw what it was. At other times I experienced variations on this same theme. Occasionally, for instance, we would be sitting at dinner in the dining-room, into the windows of which I had looked on the first night when the dream of this house visited me, but wherever we were, there was the same silence, the same sense of dreadful oppression and foreboding. And the silence I knew would always be broken by Mrs Stone saying to me, 'Jack will show you your room: I have given you the room in the tower.' Upon which (this was invariable) I had to follow him up the oak staircase with many corners, and enter the place that I dreaded more and more each time that I visited it in sleep. Or, again, I would find myself playing cards still in silence in a drawing-room lit with immense chandeliers, that gave a blinding illumination. What the game was I have no idea; what I remember, with a sense of miserable anticipation, was that soon Mrs Stone would get up and say to me, 'Jack will show you your room: I have given you the room in the tower.' This drawing-room where we played cards was next to the dining-room, and, as I have said, was always brilliantly illuminated, whereas the rest of the house was full of dusk and shadows. And yet, how often, in spite of those bouquets of lights, have I not pored over the cards that were dealt me, scarcely able for some reason to see them. Their designs, too, were strange: there were no red suits, but all were black, and among them there were certain cards which were black all over. I hated and dreaded those.

As this dream continued to recur, I got to know the greater part of the house. There was a smoking-room beyond the drawing-room, at the end of a passage with a green baize door. It was always very dark there, and as often as I went there I passed somebody whom I could not see in the doorway coming out. Curious developments, too, took place in the characters that peopled the dream as might happen to living persons. Mrs Stone, for instance, who, when I first saw her, had been black-haired, became grey, and instead of rising briskly, as she had done at first when she said, 'Jack will show you your room: I have given you the room in the tower,' got up very feebly, as if the strength was leaving her limbs. Jack also grew up, and became a rather ill-looking young man, with a brown moustache, while one of the sisters ceased to appear, and I understood she was married.

Then it so happened that I was not visited by this dream for six months or more, and I began to hope, in such inexplicable dread did I hold it, that it had passed away for good. But one night after this interval I again found myself being shown out onto the lawn for tea, and Mrs Stone was not there, while the others were all dressed in black. At once I guessed the reason, and my heart leaped at the thought that perhaps this time I should not have to sleep in the room in the tower, and though we usually all sat in silence, on this occasion the sense of relief made me talk and laugh as I had never yet done. But even then matters were not altogether comfortable, for no one else spoke, but they all looked secretly at each other. And soon the foolish stream of my talk ran dry, and gradually an apprehension worse than anything I had previously known gained on me as the light slowly faded.

Suddenly a voice which I knew well broke the stillness, the voice of Mrs Stone, saying, 'Jack will show you your room: I have given you the room in the tower.' It seemed to come from near the gate in the red-brick wall that bounded the lawn, and looking up, I saw that the grass outside was sown thick with gravestones. A curious greyish light shone from them, and I could read the lettering on the grave nearest me, and it was, 'In evil memory of Julia Stone'. And as usual Jack got up, and again I followed him through the hall and up the staircase with many corners. On this occasion it was darker than usual, and when I passed into the room in the tower I could only just see the furniture, the position of which was already familiar to me. Also there was a dreadful odour of decay in the room, and I woke screaming.

The dream, with such variations and developments as I have mentioned, went on at intervals for fifteen years. Sometimes I would dream it two or three nights in succession; once, as I have said, there was an intermission of six months, but taking a reasonable average, I should say that I dreamed it quite as often as once in a month. It had, as is plain, something of nightmare about it, since it always ended in the same appalling terror, which so far from getting less, seemed to me to gather fresh fear every time that I experienced it. There was, too, a strange and dreadful consistency about it. The characters in it, as I have mentioned, got regularly older, death and marriage visited this silent family, and I never in the dream, after Mrs Stone had died, set eyes on her again. But it was always her voice that told me that the room in the tower was prepared for me, and whether we had tea out on the lawn, or the scene was laid in one of the rooms overlooking it, I could always see her gravestone standing just outside the iron gate. It was the same, too, with the married daughter; usually she was not present, but once or twice she returned again, in company with a man, whom I took to be her husband. He, too, like the rest of them, was always silent. But, owing to the constant repetition of the dream, I had ceased to attach, in my waking hours, any significance to it. I never met Jack Stone again during all those years, nor did I ever see a house that resembled this dark house of my dream. And then something happened.

I had been in London in this year, up till the end of the July, and during the first week in August went down to stay with a friend in a house he had taken for the summer months, in the Ashdown Forest district of Sussex. I left London early, for John Clinton was to meet me at Forest Row Station, and we were going to spend the day golfing, and go to his house in the evening. He had his motor with him, and we set off, about five of the afternoon, after a thoroughly delightful day, for the drive, the distance being some ten miles. As it was still so early we did not have tea at the club house, but waited till we should get home. As we drove, the weather, which up till then had been, though hot, deliciously fresh, seemed to me to alter in quality, and become very stagnant and oppressive, and I felt that indefinable sense of ominous apprehension that I am accustomed to before thunder. John, however, did not share my views, attributing my loss of lightness to the fact that I had lost both my matches. Events proved, however, that I was right, though I do not think that the thunderstorm that broke that night was the sole cause of my depression.

Our way lay through deep high-banked lanes, and before we had gone very far I fell asleep, and was only awakened by the stopping of the motor. And with a sudden thrill, partly of fear but chiefly of curiosity, I found myself standing in the doorway of my house of dream. We went, I half wondering whether or not I was dreaming still, through a low oak-panelled hall, and out onto the lawn, where tea was laid in the shadow of the house. It was set in flower beds, a red-brick wall, with a gate in it, bounded one side, and out beyond that was a space of rough grass with a walnut tree. The façade of the house was very long, and at one end stood a three-storeyed tower, markedly older than the rest.

Here for the moment all resemblance to the repeated dream ceased. There was no silent and somehow terrible family, but a large assembly of exceedingly cheerful persons, all of whom were known to me. And in spite of the horror with which the dream itself had always filled me, I felt nothing of it now that the scene of it was thus reproduced before me. But I felt intensest curiosity as to what was going to happen.

Tea pursued its cheerful course, and before long Mrs Clinton got up. And at that moment I think I knew what she was going to say. She spoke to me, and what she said was: 'Jack will show you your room: I have given you the room in the tower.'

At that, for half a second, the horror of the dream took hold of me again. But it quickly passed, and again I felt nothing more than the most intense curiosity. It was not very long before it was amply satisfied.

John turned to me.

'Right up at the top of the house,' he said, 'but I think you'll be comfortable. We're absolutely full up. Would you like to go and see it now? By Jove, I believe that you are right, and that we are going to have a thunderstorm. How dark it has become.'

I got up and followed him. We passed through the hall, and up the perfectly familiar staircase. Then he opened the door, and I went in. And at that moment sheer unreasoning terror again possessed me. I did not know what I feared: I simply feared. Then like a sudden recollection, when one remembers a name which has long escaped the memory, I knew what I feared. I feared Mrs Stone, whose grave with the sinister inscription, 'In evil memory', I had so often seen in my dream, just beyond the lawn which lay below my window. And then once more the fear passed so completely that I wondered what there was to fear, and I found myself, sober and quiet and sane, in the room in the tower, the name of which I had so often heard in my dream, and the scene of which was so familiar.

I looked around it with a certain sense of proprietorship, and found that nothing had been changed from the dreaming nights in which I knew it so well. Just to the left of the door was the bed, lengthways along the wall, with the head of it in the angle. In a line with it was the fireplace and a small bookcase; opposite the door the outer wall was pierced by two lattice-paned windows, between which stood the dressing-table, while ranged along the fourth wall was the washing-stand and a big cupboard. My luggage had already been unpacked, for the furniture of dressing and undressing lay orderly on the wash-stand and toilet-table, while my dinner clothes were spread out on the coverlet of the bed. And then, with a sudden start of unexplained dismay, I saw that there were two rather conspicuous objects which I had not seen before in my dreams: one a life-sized oil painting of Mrs Stone, the other a black-and-white sketch of Jack Stone, representing him as he had appeared to me only a week before in the last of the series of these repeated dreams, a rather secret and evil-looking man of about thirty. His picture hung between the windows, looking straight across the room to the other portrait, which hung at the side of the bed. At that I looked next, and as I looked I felt once more the horror of nightmare seize me.

It represented Mrs Stone as I had seen her last in my dreams: old and withered and white-haired. But in spite of the evident feebleness of body, a dreadful exuberance and vitality shone through the envelope of flesh, an exuberance wholly malign, a vitality that foamed and frothed with unimaginable evil. Evil beamed from the narrow, leering eyes; it laughed in the demon-like mouth. The whole face was instinct with some secret and appalling mirth; the hands, clasped together on the knee, seemed shaking with suppressed and nameless glee. Then I saw also that it was signed in the left-hand bottom corner, and wondering who the artist could be, I looked more closely, and read the inscription, 'Julia Stone by Julia Stone'.

There came a tap at the door, and John Clinton entered.

'Got everything you want?' he asked.

'Rather more than I want,' said I, pointing to the picture.

He laughed.

'Hard-featured old lady,' he said. 'By herself, too, I remember. Anyhow she can't have flattered herself much.'

'But don't you see?' said I. 'It's scarcely a human face at all. It's the face of some witch, of some devil.'

He looked at it more closely.

'Yes; it isn't very pleasant,' he said. 'Scarcely a bedside manner, eh? Yes; I can imagine getting the nightmare if I went to sleep with that close by my bed. I'll have it taken down if you like.'

'I really wish you would,' I said.

He rang the bell, and with the help of a servant we detached the picture and carried it out onto the landing, and put it with its face to the wall.

'By Jove, the old lady is a weight,' said John, mopping his forehead. 'I wonder if she had something on her mind.'

The extraordinary weight of the picture had struck me too. I was about to reply, when I caught sight of my own hand. There was blood on it, in considerable quantities, covering the whole palm.

'I've cut myself somehow,' said I.

John gave a little startled exclamation.

'Why, I have too,' he said.

Simultaneously the footman took out his handkerchief and wiped his hand with it. I saw that there was blood also on his handkerchief.

John and I went back into the tower room and washed the blood off; but neither on his hand nor on mine was there the slightest trace of a scratch or cut. It seemed to me that, having ascertained this, we both, by a sort of tacit consent, did not allude to it again. Something in my case had dimly occurred to me that I did not wish to think about. It was but a conjecture, but I fancied that I knew the same thing had occurred to him.

The heat and oppression of the air, for the storm we had expected was still undischarged, increased very much after dinner, and for some time most of the party, among whom were John Clinton and myself, sat outside on the path bounding the lawn, where we had had tea. The night was absolutely dark, and no twinkle of star or moon ray could penetrate the pall of cloud that overset the sky. By degrees our assembly thinned, the women went up to bed, men dispersed to the smoking or billiard room, and by eleven o'clock my host and I were the only two left. All the evening I thought that he had something on his mind, and as soon as we were alone he spoke.

'The man who helped us with the picture had blood on his hand, too, did you notice?' he said.

'I asked him just now if he had cut himself, and he said he supposed he had, but that he could find no mark of it. Now where did that blood come from?'

By dint of telling myself that I was not going to think about it, I had succeeded in not doing so, and I did not want, especially just at bed-time, to be reminded of it.

'I don't know,' said I, 'and I don't really care so long as the picture of Mrs Stone is not by my bed.'

He got up.

'But it's odd,' he said. 'Ha! Now you'll see another odd thing.'

A dog of his, an Irish terrier by breed, had come out of the house as we talked. The door behind us into the hall was open, and a bright oblong of light shone across the lawn to the iron gate which led on to the rough grass outside, where the walnut tree stood. I saw that the dog had all his hackles up, bristling with rage and fright; his lips were curled back from his teeth, as if he was ready to spring at something, and he was growling to himself. He took not the slightest notice of his master or me, but stiffly and tensely walked across the grass to the iron gate. There he stood for a moment, looking through the bars and still growling. Then of a sudden his courage seemed to desert him: he gave one long howl, and scuttled back to the house with a curious crouching sort of movement.

'He does that half-a-dozen times a day,' said John. 'He sees something which he both hates and fears.'

I walked to the gate and looked over it. Something was moving on the grass outside, and soon a sound which I could not instantly identify came to my ears. Then I remembered what it was: it was the purring of a cat. I lit a match, and saw the purrer, a big blue Persian, walking round and round in a little circle just outside the gate, stepping high and ecstatically, with tail carried aloft like a banner. Its eyes were bright and shining, and every now and then it put its head down and sniffed at the grass.

I laughed.

'The end of that mystery, I am afraid,' I said. 'Here's a large cat having Walpurgis night all alone.'

'Yes, that's Darius,' said John. 'He spends half the day and all night there. But that's not the end of the dog mystery, for Toby and he are the best of friends, but the beginning of the cat mystery. What's the cat doing there? And why is Darius pleased, while Toby is terror-stricken?'

At that moment I remembered the rather horrible detail of my dreams when I saw through the gate, just where the cat was now, the white tombstone with the sinister inscription. But before I could answer the rain began, as suddenly and heavily as if a tap had been turned on, and simultaneously the big cat squeezed through the bars of the gate, and came leaping across the lawn to the house for shelter. Then it sat in the doorway, looking out eagerly into the dark. It spat and struck at John with its paw, as he pushed it in, in order to close the door.

Somehow, with the portrait of Julia Stone in the passage outside, the room in the tower had absolutely no alarm for me, and as I went to bed, feeling very sleepy and heavy, I had nothing more than interest for the curious incident about our bleeding hands, and the conduct of the cat and dog. The last thing I looked at before I put out my light was the square empty space by my bed where the portrait had been. Here the paper was of its original full tint of dark red: over the rest of the walls it had faded. Then I blew out my candle and instantly fell asleep.

My awaking was equally instantaneous, and I sat bolt upright in bed under the impression that some bright light had been flashed in my face, though it was now absolutely pitch dark. I knew exactly where I was, in the room which I had dreaded in dreams, but no horror that I ever felt when asleep approached the fear that now invaded and froze my brain. Immediately after a peal of thunder crackled just above the house, but the probability that it was only a flash of lightning which awoke me gave no reassurance to my galloping heart. Something I knew was in the room with me, and instinctively I put out my right hand, which was nearest the wall, to keep it away. And my hand touched the edge of a picture-frame hanging close to me.

I sprang out of bed, upsetting the small table that stood by it, and I heard my watch, candle, and matches clatter onto the floor. But for the moment there was no need of light, for a blinding flash leaped out of the clouds, and showed me that by my bed again hung the picture of Mrs Stone. And instantly the room went into blackness again. But in that flash I saw another thing also, namely a figure that leaned over the end of my bed, watching me. It was dressed in some close-clinging white garment, spotted and stained with mould, and the face was that of the portrait.

Overhead the thunder cracked and roared, and when it ceased and the deathly stillness succeeded, I heard the rustle of movement coming nearer me, and, more horrible yet, perceived an odour of corruption and decay. And then a hand was laid on the side of my neck, and close beside my ear I heard quick-taken, eager breathing. Yet I knew that this thing, though it could be perceived by touch, by smell, by eye and by ear, was still not of this earth, but something that had passed out of the body and had power to make itself manifest. Then a voice, already familiar to me, spoke.

'I knew you would come to the room in the tower,' it said. 'I have been long waiting for you. At last you have come. Tonight I shall feast; before long we will feast together.'

And the quick breathing came closer to me; I could feel it on my neck.

At that the terror, which I think had paralysed me for the moment, gave way to the wild instinct of self-preservation. I hit wildly with both arms, kicking out at the same moment, and heard a little animal-squeal, and something soft dropped with a thud beside me. I took a couple of steps forward, nearly tripping up over whatever it was that lay there, and by the merest good luck found the handle of the door. In another second I ran out on the landing, and had banged the door behind me. Almost at the same moment I heard a door open somewhere below, and John Clinton, candle in hand, came running upstairs.

'What is it?' he said. 'I sleep just below you, and heard a noise as if – Good heavens, there's blood on your shoulder.'

I stood there, so he told me afterwards, swaying from side to side, white as a sheet, with the mark on my shoulder as if a hand covered with blood had been laid there.

'It's in there,' I said, pointing. 'She, you know. The portrait is in there, too, hanging up on the place we took it from.'

At that he laughed.

'My dear fellow, this is mere nightmare,' he said.

He pushed by me, and opened the door, I standing there simply inert with terror, unable to stop him, unable to move.

'Phew! What an awful smell,' he said.

Then there was silence; he had passed out of my sight behind the open door. Next moment he came out again, as white as myself, and instantly shut it.

'Yes, the portrait's there,' he said, 'and on the floor is a thing – a thing spotted with earth, like what they bury people in. Come away, quick, come away.'

How I got downstairs I hardly know. An awful shuddering and nausea of the spirit rather than of the flesh had seized me, and more than once he had to place my feet upon the steps, while every now and then he cast glances of terror and apprehension up the stairs. But in time we came to his dressing-room on the floor below, and there I told him what I have here described.

The sequel can be made short; indeed, some of my readers have perhaps already guessed what it was, if they remember that inexplicable affair of the churchyard at West Fawley, some eight years ago, where an attempt was made three times to bury the body of a certain woman who had committed suicide. On each occasion the coffin was found in the course of a few days again protruding from the ground. After the third attempt, in order that the thing should not be talked about, the body was buried elsewhere in unconsecrated ground. Where it was buried was just outside the iron gate of the garden belonging to the house where this woman had lived. She had committed suicide in a room at the top of the tower in that house. Her name was Julia Stone.

Subsequently the body was again secretly dug up, and the coffin was found to be full of blood.

The Bus-Conductor

My friend, Hugh Grainger, and I had just returned from a two days' visit in the country, where we had been staying in a house of sinister repute which was supposed to be haunted by ghosts of a peculiarly fearsome and truculent sort. The house itself was all that such a house should be, Jacobean and oak-panelled, with long dark passages and high vaulted rooms. It stood, also, very remote, and was encompassed by a wood of sombre pines that muttered and whispered in the dark, and all the time that we were there a southwesterly gale with torrents of scolding rain had prevailed, so that by day and night weird voices moaned and fluted in the chimneys, a company of uneasy spirits held colloquy among the trees, and sudden tattoos and tappings beckoned from the window-panes. But in spite of these surroundings, which were sufficient in themselves, one would almost say, to spontaneously generate occult phenomena, nothing of any description had occurred. I am bound to add, also, that my own state of mind was peculiarly well adapted to receive or even to invent the sights and sounds we had gone to seek, for I was, I confess, during the whole time that we were there, in a state of abject apprehension, and lay awake both nights through hours of terrified unrest, afraid of the dark, yet more afraid of what a lighted candle might show me.

Hugh Grainger, on the evening after our return to town, had dined with me, and after dinner our conversation, as was natural, soon came back to these entrancing topics.

'But why you go ghost-seeking I cannot imagine,' he said, 'because your teeth were chattering and your eyes starting out of your head all the time you were there, from sheer fright. Or do you like being frightened?'

Hugh, though generally intelligent, is dense in certain ways; this is one of them.

'Why, of course, I like being frightened,' I said. 'I want to be made to creep and creep and creep. Fear is the most absorbing and luxurious of emotions. One forgets all else if one is afraid.'

'Well, the fact that neither of us saw anything,' he said, 'confirms what I have always believed.'

'And what have you always believed?'

'That these phenomena are purely objective, not subjective, and that one's state of mind has nothing to do with the perception that perceives them, nor have circumstances or surroundings anything to do with them either. Look at Osburton. It has had the reputation of being a haunted house for years, and it certainly has all the accessories of one. Look at yourself, too, with all your nerves on edge, afraid to look round or light a candle for fear of seeing something! Surely there was the right man in the right place then, if ghosts are subjective.'

He got up and lit a cigarette, and looking at him – Hugh is about six feet high, and as broad as he is long – I felt a retort on my lips, for I could not help my mind going back to a certain period in his life, when, from some cause which, as far as I knew, he had never told anybody, he had become a mere quivering mass of disordered nerves. Oddly enough, at the same moment and for the first time, he began to speak of it himself.

'You may reply that it was not worth my while to go either,' he said, 'because I was so clearly the wrong man in the wrong place. But I wasn't. You for all your apprehensions and expectancy have never seen a ghost. But I have, though I am the last person in the world you would have thought likely to do so, and, though my nerves are steady enough again now, it knocked me all to bits.'

He sat down again in his chair.

'No doubt you remember my going to bits,' he said, 'and since I believe that I am sound again now, I should rather like to tell you about it. But before I couldn't; I couldn't speak of it at all to anybody. Yet there ought to have been nothing frightening about it; what I saw was certainly a most useful and friendly ghost. But it came from the shaded side of things; it looked suddenly out of the night and the mystery with which life is surrounded.

'I want first to tell you quite shortly my theory about ghost-seeing,' he continued, 'and I can explain it best by a simile, an image. Imagine then that you and I and everybody in the world are like people whose eye is directly opposite a little tiny hole in a sheet of cardboard which is continually shifting and revolving and moving about. Back to back with that sheet of cardboard is another, which also, by laws of its own, is in perpetual but independent motion. In it too there is another hole, and when, fortuitously it would seem, these two holes, the one through which we are always looking, and the other in the spiritual plane, come opposite one another, we see through, and then only do the sights and sounds of the spiritual world become visible or audible to us. With most people these holes never come opposite each other during their life. But at the hour of death they do, and then they remain stationary. That, I fancy, is how we "pass over".

'Now, in some natures, these holes are comparatively large, and are constantly coming into opposition. Clairvoyants, mediums are like that. But, as far as I knew, I had no clairvoyant or mediumistic powers at all. I therefore am the sort of person who long ago made up his mind that he never would see a ghost. It was, so to speak, an incalculable chance that my minute spy-hole should come into opposition with the other. But it did: and it knocked me out of time.'

I had heard some such theory before, and though Hugh put it rather picturesquely, there was nothing in the least convincing or practical about it. It might be so, or again it might not.

'I hope your ghost was more original than your theory,' said I, in order to bring him to the point.

'Yes, I think it was. You shall judge.'

I put on more coal and poked up the fire. Hugh has got, so I have always considered, a great talent for telling stories, and that sense of drama which is so necessary for the narrator. Indeed, before now, I have suggested to him that he should take this up as a profession, sit by the fountain in Piccadilly Circus, when times are, as usual, bad, and tell stories to the passers-by in the street, Arabian fashion, for reward. The most part of mankind, I am aware, do not like long stories, but to the few, among whom I number myself, who really like to listen to lengthy accounts of experiences, Hugh is an ideal narrator. I do not care for his theories, or for his similes, but when it comes to facts, to things that happened, I like him to be lengthy.

'Go on, please, and slowly,' I said. 'Brevity may be the soul of wit, but it is the ruin of story-telling. I want to hear when and where and how it all was, and what you had for lunch and where you had dined and what – '

Hugh began.

'It was the 24th of June, just eighteen months ago,' he said. 'I had let my flat, you may remember, and came up from the country to stay with you for a week. We had dined alone here – '

I could not help interrupting.

'Did you see the ghost here?' I asked. 'In this square little box of a house in a modern street?'

'I was in the house when I saw it.'

I hugged myself in silence.

'We had dined alone here in Graeme Street,' he said, 'and after dinner I went out to some party, and you stopped at home. At dinner your man did not wait, and when I asked where he was, you told me he was ill, and, I thought, changed the subject rather abruptly. You gave me your latch-key when I went out, and on coming back, I found you had gone to bed. There were, however, several letters for me, which required answers. I wrote them there and then, and posted them at the pillar-box opposite. So I suppose it was rather late when I went upstairs.

'You had put me in the front room, on the third floor, overlooking the street, a room which I thought you generally occupied yourself. It was a very hot night, and though there had been a moon when I started to my party, on my return the whole sky was cloud-covered, and it both looked and felt as if we might have a thunderstorm before morning. I was feeling very sleepy and heavy, and it was not till after I had got into bed that I noticed by the shadows of the window-frames on the blind that only one of the windows was open. But it did not seem worth while to get out of bed in order to open it, though I felt rather airless and uncomfortable, and I went to sleep.

'What time it was when I awoke I do not know, but it was certainly not yet dawn, and I never remember being conscious of such an extraordinary stillness as prevailed. There was no sound either of foot-passengers or wheeled traffic; the music of life appeared to be absolutely mute. But now, instead of being sleepy and heavy, I felt, though I must have slept an hour or two at most, since it was not yet dawn, perfectly fresh and wide-awake, and the effort which had seemed not worth making before, that of getting out of bed and opening the other window, was quite easy now and I pulled up the blind, threw it wide open, and leaned out, for somehow I parched and pined for air. Even outside the oppression was very noticeable, and though, as you know, I am not easily given to feel the mental effects of climate, I was aware of an awful creepiness coming over me. I tried to analyse it away, but without success; the past day had been pleasant, I looked forward to another pleasant day tomorrow, and yet I was full of some nameless apprehension. I felt, too, dreadfully lonely in this stillness before the dawn.

'Then I heard suddenly and not very far away the sound of some approaching vehicle; I could distinguish the tread of two horses walking at a slow foot's pace. They were, though not yet visible, coming up the street, and yet this indication of life did not abate that dreadful sense of loneliness which I have spoken of. Also in some dim unformulated way that which was coming seemed to me to have something to do with the cause of my oppression.

'Then the vehicle came into sight. At first I could not distinguish what it was. Then I saw that the horses were black and had long tails, and that what they dragged was made of glass, but had a black frame. It was a hearse. Empty.

'It was moving up this side of the street. It stopped at your door.

'Then the obvious solution struck me. You had said at dinner that your man was ill, and you were, I thought, unwilling to speak more about his illness. No doubt, so I imagined now, he was dead, and for some reason, perhaps because you did not want me to know anything about it, you were having the body removed at night. This, I must tell you, passed through my mind quite instantaneously, and it did not occur to me how unlikely it really was, before the next thing happened.

'I was still leaning out of the window, and I remember also wondering, yet only momentarily, how odd it was that I saw things – or rather the one thing I was looking at – so very distinctly. Of course, there was a moon behind the clouds, but it was curious how every detail of the hearse and the horses was visible. There was only one man, the driver, with it, and the street was otherwise absolutely empty. It was at him I was looking now. I could see every detail of his clothes, but from where I was, so high above him, I could not see his face. He had on grey trousers, brown boots, a black coat buttoned all the way up, and a straw hat. Over his shoulder there was a strap, which seemed to support some sort of little bag. He looked exactly like – well, from my description what did he look exactly like?'

'Why – a bus-conductor,' I said instantly.

'So I thought, and even while I was thinking this, he looked up at me. He had a rather long thin face, and on his left cheek there was a mole with a growth of dark hair on it. All this was as distinct as if it had been noonday, and as if I was within a yard of him. But – so instantaneous was all that takes so long in the telling – I had not time to think it strange that the driver of a hearse should be so unfunereally dressed.

'Then he touched his hat to me, and jerked his thumb over his shoulder.

' "Just room for one inside, sir," he said.

'There was something so odious, so coarse, so unfeeling about this that I instantly drew my head in, pulled the blind down again, and then, for what reason I do not know, turned on the electric light in order to see what time it was. The hands of my watch pointed to half-past eleven.

'It was then for the first time, I think, that a doubt crossed my mind as to the nature of what I had just seen. But I put out the light again, got into bed, and began to think. We had dined; I had gone to a party, I had come back and written letters, had gone to bed and had slept. So how could it be half-past eleven? . . . . Or – *what* half-past eleven was it?

'Then another easy solution struck me; my watch must have stopped. But it had not; I could hear it ticking.

'There was stillness and silence again. I expected every moment to hear muffled footsteps on the stairs, footsteps moving slowly and smally under the weight of a heavy burden, but from inside the house there was no sound whatever. Outside, too, there was the same dead silence, while the hearse waited at the door. And the minutes ticked on and ticked on, and at length I began to see a difference in the light in the room, and knew that the dawn was beginning to break outside. But how had it happened, then, that if the corpse was to be removed at night it had not gone, and that the hearse still waited, when morning was already coming?

'Presently I got out of bed again, and with the sense of strong physical shrinking I went to the window and pulled back the blind. The dawn was coming fast; the whole street was lit by that silver hueless light of morning. But there was no hearse there.

'Once again I looked at my watch. It was just a quarter-past four. But I would swear that not half an hour had passed since it had told me that it was half-past eleven.

'Then a curious double sense, as if I was living in the present and at the same moment had been living in some other time, came over me. It was dawn on June 25th, and the street, as natural, was empty. But a little while ago the driver of a hearse had spoken to me, and it was half-past eleven. What was that driver, to what plane did he belong? And again *what* half-past eleven was it that I had seen recorded on the dial of my watch?

'And then I told myself that the whole thing had been a dream. But if you ask me whether I believed what I told myself, I must confess that I did not.

'Your man did not appear at breakfast next morning, nor did I see him again before I left that afternoon. I think if I had, I should have told you about all this, but it was still possible, you see, that what I had seen was a real hearse, driven by a real driver, for all the ghastly gaiety of the face that had looked up to mine, and the levity of his pointing hand. I might possibly have fallen asleep soon after seeing him, and slumbered through the removal of the body and the departure of the hearse. So I did not speak of it to you.'

There was something wonderfully straight-forward and prosaic in all this; here were no Jacobean houses oak-panelled and surrounded by weeping pine-trees, and somehow the very absence of suitable surroundings made the story more impressive. But for a moment a doubt assailed me.

'Don't tell me it was all a dream,' I said.

'I don't know whether it was or not. I can only say that I believe myself to have been wide awake. In any case the rest of the story is – odd.'

'I went out of town again that afternoon,' he continued, 'and I may say that I don't think that even for a moment did I get the haunting sense of what I had seen or dreamed that night out of my mind. It was present to me always as some vision unfulfilled. It was as if some clock had struck the four quarters, and I was still waiting to hear what the hour would be.

'Exactly a month afterwards I was in London again, but only for the day. I arrived at Victoria about eleven, and took the underground to Sloane Square in order to see if you were in town and would give me lunch. It was a baking hot morning, and I intended to take a bus from the King's Road as far as Graeme Street. There was one standing at the corner just as I came out of the station, but I saw that the top was full, and the inside appeared to be full also. Just as I came up to it the conductor, who, I suppose, had been inside, collecting fares or what not, came out on to the step within a few feet of me. He wore grey trousers, brown boots, a black coat buttoned, a straw hat, and over his shoulder was a strap on which hung his little machine for punching tickets. I saw his face, too; it was the face of the driver of the hearse, with a mole on the left cheek. Then he spoke to me, jerking his thumb over his shoulder.

'"Just room for one inside, sir," he said.

'At that a sort of panic-terror took possession of me, and I knew I gesticulated wildly with my arms, and cried, "No, no!" But at that moment I was living not in the hour that was then passing, but in that hour which had passed a month ago, when I leaned from the window of your bedroom here just before the dawn broke. At this moment too I knew that my spy-hole had been opposite the spy-hole into the spiritual world. What I had seen there had some significance, now being fulfilled, beyond the significance of the trivial happenings of today and tomorrow. The Powers of which we know so little were visibly working before me. And I stood there on the pavement shaking and trembling.

'I was opposite the post-office at the corner, and just as the bus started my eye fell on the clock in the window there. I need not tell you what the time was.

'Perhaps I need not tell you the rest, for you probably conjecture it, since you will not have forgotten what happened at the corner of Sloane Square at the end of July, the summer before last. The bus pulled out from the pavement into the street in order to get round a van that was standing in front of it. At the moment there came down the King's Road a big motor going at a hideously dangerous pace. It crashed full into the bus, burrowing into it as a gimlet burrows into a board.'

He paused.

'And that's my story,' he said.

Negotium Perambulans

The casual tourist in West Cornwall may just possibly have noticed, as he bowled along over the bare high plateau between Penzance and the Land's End, a dilapidated sign-post pointing down a steep lane and bearing on its battered finger the faded inscription 'Polearn 2 miles', but probably very few have had the curiosity to traverse those two miles in order to see a place to which their guide-books award so cursory a notice. It is described there, in a couple of unattractive lines, as a small fishing village with a church of no particular interest except for certain carved and painted wooden panels (originally belonging to an earlier edifice) which form an altar-rail. But the church at St Creed (the tourist is reminded) has a similar decoration far superior in point of preservation and interest, and thus even the ecclesiastically disposed are not lured to Polearn. So meagre a bait is scarce worth swallowing, and a glance at the very steep lane which in dry weather presents a carpet of sharp-pointed stones, and after rain a muddy watercourse, will almost certainly decide him not to expose his motor or his bicycle to risks like these in so sparsely populated a district. Hardly a house has met his eye since he left Penzance, and the possible trundling of a punctured bicycle for half a dozen weary miles seems a high price to pay for the sight of a few painted panels.

Polearn, therefore, even in the high noon of the tourist season, is little liable to invasion, and for the rest of the year I do not suppose that a couple of folk a day traverse those two miles (long ones at that) of steep and stony gradient. I am not forgetting the postman in this exiguous estimate, for the days are few when, leaving his pony and cart at the top of the hill, he goes as far as the village, since but a few hundred yards down the lane there stands a large white box, like a sea-trunk, by the side of the road, with a slit for letters and a locked door. Should he have in his wallet a registered letter or be the bearer of a parcel too large for insertion in the square lips of the sea-trunk, he must needs trudge down the hill and deliver the troublesome missive, leaving it in person on the owner, and receiving some small reward of coin or refreshment for his kindness. But such occasions are rare, and his general routine is to take out of the box such letters as may have been deposited there, and insert in their place such letters as he has brought. These will be called for, perhaps that day or perhaps the next, by an emissary from the Polearn post-office. As for the fishermen of the place, who, in their export trade, constitute the chief link of movement between Polearn and the outside world, they would not dream of taking their catch up the steep lane and so, with six miles farther of travel, to the market at Penzance. The sea route is shorter and easier, and they deliver their wares to the pier-head. Thus, though the sole industry of Polearn is sea-fishing, you will get no fish there unless you have bespoken your requirements to one of the fishermen. Back come the trawlers as empty as a haunted house, while their spoils are in the fish-train that is speeding to London.

Such isolation of a little community, continued, as it has been, for centuries, produces isolation in the individual as well, and nowhere will you find greater independence of character than among the people of Polearn. But they are linked together, so it has always seemed to me, by some mysterious comprehension: it is as if they had all been initiated into some ancient rite, inspired and framed by forces visible and invisible. The winter storms that batter the coast, the vernal spell of the spring, the hot, still summers, the season of rains and autumnal decay, have made a spell which, line by line, has been communicated to them, concerning the powers, evil and good, that rule the world, and manifest themselves in ways benignant or terrible . . . .

I came to Polearn first at the age of ten, a small boy, weak and sickly, and threatened with pulmonary trouble. My father's business kept him in London, while for me abundance of fresh air and a mild climate were considered essential conditions if I was to grow to manhood. His sister had married the vicar of Polearn, Richard Bolitho, himself native to the place, and so it came about that I spent three years, as a paying guest, with my relations. Richard Bolitho owned a fine house in the place, which he inhabited in preference to the vicarage, which he let to a young artist, John Evans, on whom the spell of Polearn had fallen for from year's beginning to year's end he never left it. There was a solid roofed shelter, open on one side to the air, built for me in the garden, and here I lived and slept, passing scarcely one hour out of the twenty-four behind walls and windows. I was out on the bay with the fisher-folk, or wandering along the gorse-clad cliffs that climbed steeply to right and left of the deep combe where the village lay, or pottering about on the pier-head, or bird's-nesting in the bushes with the boys of the village. Except on Sunday and for the few daily hours of my lessons, I might do what I pleased so long as I remained in the open air. About the lessons there was nothing formidable; my uncle conducted me through flowering bypaths among the thickets of arithmetic, and made pleasant excursions into the elements of Latin grammar, and above all, he made me daily give him an account, in clear and grammatical sentences, of what had been occupying my mind or my movements. Should I select to tell him about a walk along the cliffs, my speech must be orderly, not vague, slip-shod notes of what I had observed. In this way, too, he trained my observation, for he would bid me tell him what flowers were in bloom, and what birds hovered fishing over the sea or were building in the bushes. For that I owe him a perennial gratitude, for to observe and to express my thoughts in the clear spoken word became my life's profession.

But far more formidable than my weekday tasks was the prescribed routine for Sunday. Some dark embers compounded of Calvinism and mysticism smouldered in my uncle's soul, and made it a day of terror. His sermon in the morning scorched us with a foretaste of the eternal fires reserved for unrepentant sinners, and he was hardly less terrifying at the children's service in the afternoon. Well do I remember his exposition of the doctrine of guardian angels. A child, he said, might think himself secure in such angelic care, but let him beware of committing any of those numerous offences which would cause his guardian to turn his face from him, for as sure as there were angels to protect us, there were also evil and awful presences which were ready to pounce; and on them he dwelt with peculiar gusto. Well, too, do I remember in the morning sermon his commentary on the carved panels of the altar-rails to which I have already alluded. There was the angel of the Annunciation there, and the angel of the Resurrection, but not less was there the witch of Endor, and, on the fourth panel, a scene that concerned me most of all. This fourth panel (he came down from his pulpit to trace its time-worn features) represented the lych-gate of the churchyard at Polearn itself, and indeed the resemblance when thus pointed out was remarkable. In the entry stood the figure of a robed priest holding up a Cross, with which he faced a terrible creature like a gigantic slug, that reared itself up in front of him. That, so ran my uncle's interpretation, was some evil agency, such as he had spoken about to us children, of almost infinite malignity and power, which could alone be combated by firm faith and a pure heart. Below ran the legend '*Negotium perambulans in tenebris*' from the ninety-first Psalm. We should find it translated there, 'the pestilence that walketh in darkness', which but feebly rendered the Latin. It was more deadly to the soul than any pestilence that can only kill the body: it was the Thing, the Creature, the Business that trafficked in the outer Darkness, a minister of God's wrath on the unrighteous . . . .

I could see, as he spoke, the looks which the congregation exchanged with each other, and knew that his words were evoking a surmise, a remembrance. Nods and whispers passed between them, they understood to what he alluded, and with the inquisitiveness of boyhood I could not rest till I had wormed the story out of my friends among the fisher-boys, as, next morning, we sat basking and naked in the sun after our bathe. One knew one bit of it, one another, but it pieced together into a truly alarming legend. In bald outline it was as follows.

A church far more ancient than that in which my uncle terrified us every Sunday had once stood not three hundred yards away, on the shelf of level ground below the quarry from which its stones were hewn. The owner of the land had pulled this down, and erected for himself a house on the same site out of these materials, keeping, in a very ecstasy of wickedness, the altar, and on this he dined and played dice afterwards. But as he grew old some black melancholy seized him, and he would have lights burning there all night, for he had deadly fear of the darkness. On one winter evening there sprang up such a gale as was never before known, which broke in the windows of the room where he had supped, and extinguished the lamps. Yells of terror brought in his servants, who found him lying on the floor with the blood streaming from his throat. As they entered some huge black shadow seemed to move away from him, crawled across the floor and up the wall and out of the broken window.

'There he lay a-dying,' said the last of my informants, 'and him that had been a great burly man was withered to a bag o' skin, for the critter had drained all the blood from him. His last breath was a scream, and he hollered out the same words as passon read off the screen.'

'*Negotium perambulans in tenebris*,' I suggested eagerly.

'Thereabouts. Latin anyhow.'

'And after that?' I asked.

'Nobody would go near the place, and the old house rotted and fell in ruins till three years ago, when along comes Mr Dooliss from Penzance, and built the half of it up again. But he don't care much about such critters, nor about Latin neither. He takes his bottle of whisky a day and gets drunk's a lord in the evening. Eh, I'm gwine home to my dinner.'

Whatever the authenticity of the legend, I had certainly heard the truth about Mr Dooliss from Penzance, who from that day became an object of keen curiosity on my part, the more so because the quarry-house adjoined my uncle's garden. The Thing that walked in the dark failed to stir my imagination, and already I was so used to sleeping alone in my shelter that the night had no terrors for me. But it would be intensely exciting to wake at some timeless hour and hear Mr Dooliss yelling, and conjecture that the Thing had got him.

But by degrees the whole story faded from my mind, overscored by the more vivid interests of the day, and, for the last two years of my outdoor life in the vicarage garden, I seldom thought about Mr Dooliss and the possible fate that might await him for his temerity in living in the place where that Thing of darkness had done business. Occasionally I saw him over the garden fence, a great yellow lump of a man, with slow and staggering gait, but never did I set eyes on him outside his gate, either in the village street or down on the beach. He interfered with none, and no one interfered with him. If he wanted to run the risk of being the prey of the legendary nocturnal monster, or quietly drink himself to death, it was his affair. My uncle, so I gathered, had made several attempts to see him when first he came to live at Polearn, but Mr Dooliss appeared to have no use for parsons, but said he was not at home and never returned the call.

After three years of sun, wind, and rain, I had completely outgrown my early symptoms and had become a tough, strapping youngster of thirteen. I was sent to Eton and Cambridge, and in due course ate my dinners and became a barrister. In twenty years from that time I was earning a yearly income of five figures, and had already laid by in sound securities a sum that brought me dividends which would, for one of my simple tastes and frugal habits, supply me with all the material comforts I needed on this side of the grave. The great prizes of my profession were already within my reach, but I had no ambition beckoning me on, nor did I want a wife and children, being, I must suppose, a natural celibate. In fact there was only one ambition which through these busy years had held the lure of blue and far-off hills to me, and that was to get back to Polearn, and live once more isolated from the world with the sea and the gorse-clad hills for playfellows, and the secrets that lurked there for exploration. The spell of it had been woven about my heart, and I can truly say that there had hardly passed a day in all those years in which the thought of it and the desire for it had been wholly absent from my mind. Though I had been in frequent communication with my uncle there during his lifetime, and, after his death, with his widow who still lived there, I had never been back to it since I embarked on my profession, for I knew that if I went there, it would be a wrench beyond my power to tear myself away again. But I had made up my mind that when once I had provided for my own independence, I would go back there not to leave it again. And yet I did leave it again, and now nothing in the world would induce me to turn down the lane from the road that leads from Penzance to the Land's End, and see the sides of the combe rise steep above the roofs of the village and hear the gulls chiding as they fish in the bay. One of the things invisible, of the dark powers, leaped into light, and I saw it with my eyes.

The house where I had spent those three years of boyhood had been left for life to my aunt, and when I made known to her my intention of coming back to Polearn, she suggested that, till I found a suitable house or found her proposal unsuitable, I should come to live with her.

'The house is too big for a lone old woman,' she wrote, 'and I have often thought of quitting and taking a little cottage sufficient for me and my requirements. But come and share it, my dear, and if you find me troublesome, you or I can go. You may want solitude – most people in Polearn do – and will leave me. Or else I will leave you: one of the main reasons of my stopping here all these years was a feeling that I must not let the old house starve. Houses starve, you know, if they are not lived in. They die a lingering death; the spirit in them grows weaker and weaker, and at last fades out of them. Isn't this nonsense to your London notions? . . .'

Naturally I accepted with warmth this tentative arrangement, and on an evening in June found myself at the head of the lane leading down to Polearn, and once more I descended into the steep valley between the hills. Time had stood still apparently for the combe, the dilapidated signpost (or its successor) pointed a rickety finger down the lane, and a few hundred yards farther on was the white box for the exchange of letters. Point after remembered point met my eye, and what I saw was not shrunk, as is often the case with the revisited scenes of childhood, into a smaller scale. There stood the post-office, and there the church and close beside it the vicarage, and beyond, the tall shrubberies which separated the house for which I was bound from the road, and beyond that again the grey roofs of the quarry-house damp and shining with the moist evening wind from the sea. All was exactly as I remembered it, and, above all, that sense of seclusion and isolation. Somewhere above the tree-tops climbed the lane which joined the main road to Penzance, but all that had become immeasurably distant. The years that had passed since last I turned in at the well-known gate faded like a frosty breath, and vanished in this warm, soft air. There were law-courts somewhere in memory's dull book which, if I cared to turn the pages, would tell me that I had made a name and a great income there. But the dull book was closed now, for I was back in Polearn, and the spell was woven around me again.

And if Polearn was unchanged, so too was Aunt Hester, who met me at the door. Dainty and china-white she had always been, and the years had not aged but only refined her. As we sat and talked after dinner she spoke of all that had happened in Polearn in that score of years, and yet somehow the changes of which she spoke seemed but to confirm the immutability of it all. As the recollection of names came back to me, I asked her about the quarry-house and Mr Dooliss, and her face gloomed a little as with the shadow of a cloud on a spring day.

'Yes, Mr Dooliss,' she said, 'poor Mr Dooliss, how well I remember him, though it must be ten years and more since he died. I never wrote to you about it, for it was all very dreadful, my dear, and I did not want to darken your memories of Polearn. Your uncle always thought that something of the sort might happen if he went on in his wicked, drunken ways, and worse than that, and though nobody knew exactly what took place, it was the sort of thing that might have been anticipated.'

'But what more or less happened, Aunt Hester?' I asked.

'Well, of course I can't tell you everything, for no one knew it. But he was a very sinful man, and the scandal about him at Newlyn was shocking. And then he lived, too, in the quarry-house . . . I wonder if by any chance you remember a sermon of your uncle's when he got out of the pulpit and explained that panel in the altar-rails, the one, I mean, with the horrible creature rearing itself up outside the lych-gate?'

'Yes, I remember perfectly,' said I.

'Ah. It made an impression on you, I suppose, and so it did on all who heard him, and that impression got stamped and branded on us all when the catastrophe occurred. Somehow Mr Dooliss got to hear about your uncle's sermon, and in some drunken fit he broke into the church and smashed the panel to atoms. He seems to have thought that there was some magic in it, and that if he destroyed that he would get rid of the terrible fate that was threatening him. For I must tell you that before he committed that dreadful sacrilege he had been a haunted man: he hated and feared darkness, for he thought that the creature on the panel was on his track, but that as long as he kept lights burning it could not touch him. But the panel, to his disordered mind, was the root of his terror, and so, as I said, he broke into the church and attempted – you will see why I said "attempted" – to destroy it. It certainly was found in splinters next morning, when your uncle went into church for matins, and knowing Mr Dooliss's fear of the panel, he went across to the quarry-house afterwards and taxed him with its destruction. The man never denied it; he boasted of what he had done. There he sat, though it was early morning, drinking his whisky.

' "I've settled your Thing for you," he said, "and your sermon too. A fig for such superstitions."

'Your uncle left him without answering his blasphemy, meaning to go straight into Penzance and give information to the police about this outrage to the church, but on his way back from the quarry-house he went into the church again, in order to be able to give details about the damage, and there in the screen was the panel, untouched and uninjured. And yet he had himself seen it smashed, and Mr Dooliss had confessed that the destruction of it was his work. But there it was, and whether the power of God had mended it or some other power, who knows?'

This was Polearn indeed, and it was the spirit of Polearn that made me accept all Aunt Hester was telling me as attested fact. It had happened like that. She went on in her quiet voice.

'Your uncle recognised that some power beyond police was at work, and he did not go to Penzance or give information about the outrage, for the evidence of it had vanished.'

A sudden spate of scepticism swept over me.

'There must have been some mistake,' I said. 'It hadn't been broken . . . .'

She smiled.

'Yes, my dear, but you have been in London so long,' she said. 'Let me, anyhow, tell you the rest of my story. That night, for some reason, I could not sleep. It was very hot and airless; I dare say you will think that the sultry conditions accounted for my wakefulness. Once and again, as I went to the window to see if I could not admit more air, I could see from it the quarry-house, and I noticed the first time that I left my bed that it was blazing with lights. But the second time I saw that it was all in darkness, and as I wondered at that, I heard a terrible scream, and the moment afterwards the steps of someone coming at full speed down the road outside the gate. He yelled as he ran; "Light, light!" he called out. "Give me light, or it will catch me!" It was very terrible to hear that, and I went to rouse my husband, who was sleeping in the dressing-room across the passage. He wasted no time, but by now the whole village was aroused by the screams, and when he got down to the pier he found that all was over. The tide was low, and on the rocks at its foot was lying the body of Mr Dooliss. He must have cut some artery when he fell on those sharp edges of stone, for he had bled to death, they thought, and though he was a big burly man, his corpse was but skin and bones. Yet there was no pool of blood round him, such as you would have expected. Just skin and bones as if every drop of blood in his body had been sucked out of him!'

She leaned forward.

'You and I, my dear, know what happened,' she said, 'or at least can guess. God has His instruments of vengeance on those who bring wickedness into places that have been holy. Dark and mysterious are His ways.'

Now what I should have thought of such a story if it had been told me in London I can easily imagine. There was such an obvious explanation: the man in question had been a drunkard, what wonder if the demons of delirium pursued him? But here in Polearn it was different.

'And who is in the quarry-house now?' I asked. 'Years ago the fisher-boys told me the story of the man who first built it and of his horrible end. And now again it has happened. Surely no one has ventured to inhabit it once more?'

I saw in her face, even before I asked that question, that somebody had done so.

'Yes, it is lived in again,' said she, 'for there is no end to the blindness . . . I don't know if you remember him. He was tenant of the vicarage many years ago.'

'John Evans,' said I.

'Yes. Such a nice fellow he was too. Your uncle was pleased to get so good a tenant. And now – '

She rose.

'Aunt Hester, you shouldn't leave your sentences unfinished,' I said.

She shook her head.

'My dear, that sentence will finish itself,' she said. 'But what a time of night! I must go to bed, and you too, or they will think we have to keep lights burning here through the dark hours.'

Before getting into bed I drew my curtains wide and opened all the windows to the warm tide of the sea air that flowed softly in. Looking out into the garden I could see in the moonlight the roof of the shelter, in which for three years I had lived, gleaming with dew. That, as much as anything, brought back the old days to which I had now returned, and they seemed of one piece with the present, as if no gap of more than twenty years sundered them. The two flowed into one like globules of mercury uniting into a softly shining globe, of mysterious lights and reflections. Then, raising my eyes a little, I saw against the black hill-side the windows of the quarry-house still alight.

Morning, as is so often the case, brought no shattering of my illusion. As I began to regain consciousness, I fancied that I was a boy again waking up in the shelter in the garden, and though, as I grew more widely awake, I smiled at the impression, that on which it was based I found to be indeed true. It was sufficient now as then to be here, to wander again on the cliffs, and hear the popping of the ripened seed-pods on the gorse-bushes; to stray along the shore to the bathing-cove, to float and drift and swim in the warm tide, and bask on the sand, and watch the gulls fishing, to lounge on the pier-head with the fisher-folk, to see in their eyes and hear in their quiet speech the evidence of secret things not so much known to them as part of their instincts and their very being. There were powers and presences about me; the white poplars that stood by the stream that babbled down the valley knew of them, and showed a glimpse of their knowledge sometimes, like the gleam of their white under-leaves; the very cobbles that paved the street were soaked in it . . . . All that I wanted was to lie there and grow soaked in it too; unconsciously, as a boy, I had done that, but now the process must be conscious. I must know what stir of forces, fruitful and mysterious, seethed along the hill-side at noon, and sparkled at night on the sea. They could be known, they could even be controlled by those who were masters of the spell, but never could they be spoken of, for they were dwellers in the innermost, grafted into the eternal life of the world. There were dark secrets as well as these clear, kindly powers, and to these no doubt belonged the *negotium perambulans in tenebris* which, though of deadly malignity, might be regarded not only as evil, but as the avenger of sacrilegious and impious deeds . . . . All this was part of the spell of Polearn, of which the seeds had long lain dormant in me. But now they were sprouting, and who knew what strange flower would unfold on their stems?

It was not long before I came across John Evans. One morning, as I lay on the beach, there came shambling across the sand a man stout and middle-aged with the face of Silenus. He paused as he drew near and regarded me from narrow eyes.

'Why, you're the little chap that used to live in the parson's garden,' he said. 'Don't you recognise me?'

I saw who it was when he spoke: his voice, I think, instructed me, and recognising it, I could see the features of the strong, alert young man in this gross caricature.

'Yes, you're John Evans,' I said. 'You used to be very kind to me: you used to draw pictures for me.'

'So I did, and I'll draw you some more. Been bathing? That's a risky performance. You never know what lives in the sea, nor what lives on the land for that matter. Not that I heed them. I stick to work and whisky. God! I've learned to paint since I saw you, and drink too for that matter. I live in the quarry-house, you know, and it's a powerful thirsty place. Come and have a look at my things if you're passing. Staying with your aunt, are you? I could do a wonderful portrait of her. Interesting face; she knows a lot. People who live at Polearn get to know a lot, though I don't take much stock in that sort of knowledge myself.'

I do not know when I have been at once so repelled and interested. Behind the mere grossness of his face there lurked something which, while it appalled, yet fascinated me. His thick lisping speech had the same quality. And his paintings, what would they be like? . . . .

'I was just going home,' I said. 'I'll gladly come in, if you'll allow me.'

He took me through the untended and overgrown garden into the house which I had never yet entered. A great grey cat was sunning itself in the window, and an old woman was laying lunch in a corner of the cool hall into which the door opened. It was built of stone, and the carved mouldings let into the walls, the fragments of gargoyles and sculptured images, bore testimony to the truth of its having been built out of the demolished church. In one corner was an oblong and carved wooden table littered with a painter's apparatus and stacks of canvases leaned against the walls.

He jerked his thumb towards a head of an angel that was built into the mantelpiece and giggled.

'Quite a sanctified air,' he said, 'so we tone it down for the purposes of ordinary life by a different sort of art. Have a drink? No? Well, turn over some of my pictures while I put myself to rights.'

He was justified in his own estimate of his skill: he could paint (and apparently he could paint anything), but never have I seen pictures so inexplicably hellish. There were exquisite studies of trees, and you knew that something lurked in the flickering shadows. There was a drawing of his cat sunning itself in the window, even as I had just now seen it, and yet it was no cat but some beast of awful malignity. There was a boy stretched naked on the sands, not human, but some evil thing which had come out of the sea. Above all there were pictures of his garden overgrown and jungle-like, and you knew that in the bushes were presences ready to spring out on you . . . .

'Well, do you like my style?' he said as he came up, glass in hand. (The tumbler of spirits that he held had not been diluted.) 'I try to paint the essence of what I see, not the mere husk and skin of it, but its nature, where it comes from and what gave it birth. There's much in common between a cat and a fuchsia-bush if you look at them closely enough. Everything came out of the slime of the pit, and it's all going back there. I should like to do a picture of you some day. I'd hold the mirror up to Nature, as that old lunatic said.'

After this first meeting I saw him occasionally throughout the months of that wonderful summer. Often he kept to his house and to his painting for days together, and then perhaps some evening I would find him lounging on the pier, always alone, and every time we met thus the repulsion and interest grew, for every time he seemed to have gone farther along a path of secret knowledge towards some evil shrine where complete initiation awaited him . . . . And then suddenly the end came.

I had met him thus one evening on the cliffs while the October sunset still burned in the sky, but over it with amazing rapidity there spread from the west a great blackness of cloud such as I have never seen for denseness. The light was sucked from the sky, the dusk fell in ever thicker layers. He suddenly became conscious of this.

'I must get back as quick as I can,' he said. 'It will be dark in a few minutes, and my servant is out. The lamps will not be lit.'

He stepped out with extraordinary briskness for one who shambled and could scarcely lift his feet, and soon broke out into a stumbling run. In the gathering darkness I could see that his face was moist with the dew of some unspoken terror.

'You must come with me,' he panted, 'for so we shall get the lights burning the sooner. I cannot do without light.'

I had to exert myself to the full to keep up with him, for terror winged him, and even so I fell behind, so that when I came to the garden gate, he was already half-way up the path to the house. I saw him enter, leaving the door wide, and found him fumbling with matches. But his hand so trembled that he could not transfer the light to the wick of the lamp.

'But what's the hurry about?' I asked.

Suddenly his eyes focused themselves on the open door behind me, and he jumped from his seat beside the table which had once been the altar of God, with a gasp and a scream.

'No, no!' he cried. 'Keep it off! . . . .'

I turned and saw what he had seen. The Thing had entered and now was swiftly sliding across the floor towards him, like some gigantic caterpillar. A stale phosphorescent light came from it, for though the dusk had grown to blackness outside, I could see it quite distinctly in the awful light of its own presence. From it too there came an odour of corruption and decay, as from slime that has long lain below water. It seemed to have no head, but on the front of it was an orifice of puckered skin which opened and shut and slavered at the edges. It was hairless, and slug-like in shape and in texture. As it advanced its fore-part reared itself from the ground, like a snake about to strike, and it fastened on him . . . .

At that sight, and with the yells of his agony in my ears, the panic which had struck me relaxed into a hopeless courage, and with palsied, impotent hands I tried to lay hold of the Thing. But I could not: though something material was there, it was impossible to grasp it; my hands sunk in it as in thick mud. It was like wrestling with a nightmare.

I think that but a few seconds elapsed before all was over. The screams of the wretched man sank to moans and mutterings as the Thing fell on him: he panted once or twice and was still. For a moment longer there came gurglings and sucking noises, and then it slid out even as it had entered. I lit the lamp which he had fumbled with, and there on the floor he lay, no more than a rind of skin in loose folds over projecting bones.

'And No Bird Sings'

The red chimneys of the house for which I was bound were visible from just outside the station at which I had alighted, and, so the chauffeur told me, the distance was not more than a mile's walk if I took the path across the fields. It ran straight till it came to the edge of that wood yonder, which belonged to my host, and above which his chimneys were visible. I should find a gate in the paling of this wood, and a track traversing it, which debouched close to his garden. So, on this adorable afternoon of early May, it seemed a waste of time to do other than walk through meadows and woods, and I set off on foot, while the motor carried my traps.

It was one of those golden days which every now and again leak out of paradise and drip to earth. Spring had been late in coming, but now it was here with a burst, and the whole world was boiling with the sap of life. Never have I seen such a wealth of spring flowers, or such vividness of green, or heard such melodious business among the birds in the hedgerows; this walk through the meadows was a jubilee of festal ecstasy. And best of all, so I promised myself, would be the passage through the wood newly fledged with milky green that lay just ahead. There was the gate, just facing me, and I passed through it into the dappled lights and shadows of the grass-grown track.

Coming out of the brilliant sunshine was like entering a dim tunnel; one had the sense of being suddenly withdrawn from the brightness of the spring into some subaqueous cavern. The tree-tops formed a green roof overhead, excluding the light to a remarkable degree. I moved in a world of shifting obscurity. Presently, as the trees grew more scattered, their place was taken by a thick growth of hazels, which met over the path, and then, the ground sloping downwards, I came upon an open clearing, covered with bracken and heather, and studded with birches. But though now I walked once more beneath the luminous sky, with the sunlight pouring down, it seemed to have lost its effulgence. The brightness – was it some odd optical illusion? – was veiled as if it came from crape. Yet there was the sun still well above the tree-tops in an unclouded heaven, but for all that the light was that of a stormy winter's day, without warmth or brilliance. It was oddly silent too; I had thought that the bushes and trees would be ringing with the song of mating-birds, but listening, I could hear no note of any sort, neither the fluting of thrush or blackbird, nor the cheerful whirr of the chaffinch, nor the cooing wood-pigeon, nor the strident clamour of the jay. I paused to verify this odd silence; there was no doubt about it. It was rather eerie, rather uncanny, but I supposed the birds knew their own business best, and if they were too busy to sing it was their affair.

As I went on it struck me also that since entering the wood I had not seen a bird of any kind; and now, as I crossed the clearing, I kept my eyes alert for them, but fruitlessly, and soon I entered the further belt of thick trees which surrounded it. Most of them I noticed were beeches, growing very close to each other, and the ground beneath them was bare but for the carpet of fallen leaves, and a few thin bramble-bushes. In this curious dimness and thickness of the trees, it was impossible to see far to right or left of the path, and now, for the first time since I had left the open, I heard some sound of life. There came the rustle of leaves from not far away, and I thought to myself that a rabbit, anyhow, was moving. But somehow it lacked the staccato patter of a small animal; there was a certain stealthy heaviness about it, as if something much larger were stealing along and desirous of not being heard. I paused again to see what might emerge, but instantly the sound ceased. Simultaneously I was conscious of some faint but very foul odour reaching me, a smell choking and corrupt, yet somehow pungent, more like the odour of something alive rather than rotting. It was peculiarly sickening, and not wanting to get any closer to its source, I went on my way.

Before long I came to the edge of the wood; straight in front of me was a strip of meadow-land, and beyond an iron gate between two brick walls, through which I had a glimpse of lawn and flower beds. To the left stood the house, and over house and garden there poured the amazing brightness of the declining afternoon.

Hugh Granger and his wife were sitting out on the lawn, with the usual pack of assorted dogs: a Welsh collie, a yellow retriever, a fox-terrier, and a Pekinese. Their protest at my intrusion gave way to the welcome of recognition, and I was admitted into the circle. There was much to say, for I had been out of England for the last three months, during which time Hugh had settled into this little estate left him by a recluse uncle, and he and Daisy had been busy during the Easter vacation with getting into the house. Certainly it was a most attractive legacy; the house, through which I was presently taken, was a delightful little Queen Anne manor, and its situation on the edge of this heather-clad Surrey ridge quite superb. We had tea in a small panelled parlour overlooking the garden, and soon the wider topics narrowed down to those of the day and the hour. I had walked, had I, asked Daisy, from the station: did I go through the wood, or follow the path outside it?

The question she thus put to me was given trivially enough; there was no hint in her voice that it mattered a straw to her which way I had come. But it was quite clearly borne in upon me that not only she but Hugh also listened intently for my reply. He had just lit a match for his cigarette, but held it unapplied till he heard my answer. Yes, I had gone through the wood; but now, though I had received some odd impressions in the wood, it seemed quite ridiculous to mention what they were. I could not soberly say that the sunshine there was of very poor quality, and that at one point in my traverse I had smelt a most iniquitous odour. I had walked through the wood; that was all I had to tell them.

I had known both my host and hostess for a tale of many years, and now, when I felt that there was nothing except purely fanciful stuff that I could volunteer about my experiences there, I noticed that they exchanged a swift glance, and could easily interpret it. Each of them signalled to the other an expression of relief; they told each other (so I construed their glance) that I, at any rate, had found nothing unusual in the wood, and they were pleased at that. But then, before any real pause had succeeded to my answer that I had gone through the wood, I remembered that strange absence of birdsong and bird, and as that seemed an innocuous observation in natural history, I thought I might as well mention it.

'One odd thing struck me,' I began (and instantly I saw the attention of both riveted again), 'I didn't see a single bird or hear one from the time I entered the wood to when I left it.'

Hugh lit his cigarette.

'I've noticed that too,' he said, 'and it's rather puzzling. The wood is certainly a bit of primeval forest, and one would have thought that hosts of birds would have nested in it from time immemorial. But, like you, I've never heard or seen one in it. And I've never seen a rabbit there either.'

'I thought I heard one this afternoon,' said I. 'Something was moving in the fallen beech-leaves.'

'Did you see it?' he asked.

I recollected that I had decided that the noise was not quite the patter of a rabbit.

'No, I didn't see it,' I said, 'and perhaps it wasn't one. It sounded, I remember, more like something larger.'

Once again and unmistakably a glance passed between Hugh and his wife, and she rose.

'I must be off,' she said. 'Post goes out at seven, and I lazed all morning. What are you two going to do?'

'Something out of doors, please,' said I. 'I want to see the domain.'

Hugh and I accordingly strolled out again with the cohort of dogs. The domain was certainly very charming; a small lake lay beyond the garden, with a reed bed vocal with warblers, and a tufted margin into which coots and moorhens scudded at our approach. Rising from the end of that was a high heathery knoll full of rabbit holes, which the dogs nosed at with joyful expectations, and there we sat for a while overlooking the wood which covered the rest of the estate. Even now, in the blaze of the sun near to its setting, it seemed to be in shadow, though like the rest of the view it should have basked in brilliance, for not a cloud flecked the sky and the level rays enveloped the world in a crimson splendour. But the wood was grey and darkling. Hugh, also, I was aware, had been looking at it, and now, with an air of breaking into a disagreeable topic, he turned to me.

'Tell me,' he said, 'does anything strike you about that wood?'

'Yes: it seems to lie in shadow.'

He frowned.

'But it can't, you know,' he said. 'Where does the shadow come from? Not from outside, for sky and land are on fire.'

'From inside, then?' I asked.

He was silent a moment.

'There's something queer about it,' he said at length. 'There's something there, and I don't know what it is. Daisy feels it too; she won't ever go into the wood, and it appears that birds won't either. Is it just the fact that, for some unexplained reason, there are no birds in it that has set all our imaginations at work?'

I jumped up.

'Oh, it's all rubbish,' I said. 'Let's go through it now and find a bird. I bet you I find a bird.'

'Sixpence for every bird you see,' said Hugh.

We went down the hillside and walked round the wood till we came to the gate where I had entered that afternoon. I held it open after I had gone in for the dogs to follow. But there they stood, a yard or so away, and none of them moved.

'Come on, dogs,' I said, and Fifi, the fox-terrier, came a step nearer and then, with a little whine, retreated again.

'They always do that,' said Hugh; 'not one of them will set foot inside the wood. Look!'

He whistled and called, he cajoled and scolded, but it was no use. There the dogs remained, with little apologetic grins and signallings of tails, but quite determined not to come.

'But why?' I asked.

'Same reason as the birds, I suppose, whatever that happens to be. There's Fifi, for instance, the sweetest-tempered little lady; once I tried to pick her up and carry her in, and she snapped at me. They'll have nothing to do with the wood; they'll trot round outside it and go home.'

We left them there and, in the sunset light which was now beginning to fade, began the passage. Usually the sense of eeriness disappears if one has a companion, but now to me, even with Hugh walking by my side, the place seemed even more uncanny than it had done that afternoon, and a sense of intolerable uneasiness, that grew into a sort of waking nightmare, obsessed me. I had thought before that the silence and loneliness of it had played tricks with my nerves; but with Hugh here it could not be that, and indeed I felt that it was not any such notion that lay at the root of this fear, but rather the conviction that there was some presence lurking there, invisible as yet, but permeating the gathered gloom. I could not form the slightest idea of what it might be, or whether it was material or ghostly; all I could diagnose of it from my own sensations was that it was evil and antique.

As we came to the open ground in the middle of the wood, Hugh stopped, and though the evening was cool I noticed that he mopped his forehead.

'Pretty nasty,' he said. 'No wonder the dogs don't like it. How do you feel about it?'

Before I could answer he shot out his hand, pointing to the belt of trees that lay beyond.

'What's that?' he said in whisper.

I followed his finger, and for one half-second thought I saw against the black of the wood some vague flicker, grey or faintly luminous. It waved as if it had been the head and forepart of some huge snake rearing itself, but it instantly disappeared, and my glimpse had been so momentary that I could not trust my impression.

'It's gone,' said Hugh, still looking in the direction he had pointed; and as we stood there I heard again what I had heard that afternoon, a rustle among the fallen beech-leaves. But there was no wind nor breath of breeze astir.

He turned to me.

'What on earth was it?' he said. 'It looked like some enormous slug standing up. Did you see it?'

'I'm not sure whether I did or not,' I said. 'I think I just caught sight of what you saw.'

'But what was it?' he said again. 'Was it a real material creature, or was it – '

'Something ghostly, do you mean?' I asked.

'Something half-way between the two,' he said. 'I'll tell you what I mean afterwards, when we've got out of this place.'

The thing, whatever it was, had vanished among the trees to the left of where our path lay, and in silence we walked across the open till we came to where it entered tunnel-like among the trees. Frankly I hated and feared the thought of plunging into that darkness with the knowledge that not so far off there was something the nature of which I could not ever so faintly conjecture, but which, I now made no doubt, was that which filled the wood with some nameless terror. Was it material, was it ghostly, or was it (and now some inkling of what Hugh meant began to form itself into my mind) some being that lay on the borderland between the two? Of all the sinister possibilities that appeared the most terrifying.

As we entered the trees again I perceived that reek, alive and yet corrupt, which I had smelt before, but now it was far more potent, and we hurried on, choking with the odour that I now guessed to be not the putrescence of decay, but the living substance of that which crawled and reared itself in the darkness of the wood where no bird would shelter. Somewhere among those trees lurked the reptilian thing that defied and yet compelled credence.

It was a blessed relief to get out of that dim tunnel into the wholesome air of the open and the clear light of evening. Within doors, when we returned, windows were curtained and lamps lit. There was a hint of frost, and Hugh put a match to the fire in his room, where the dogs, still a little apologetic, hailed us with thumpings of drowsy tails.

'And now we've got to talk,' said he, 'and lay our plans, for whatever it is that is in the wood we've got to make an end of it. And, if you want to know what I think it is, I'll tell you.'

'Go ahead,' said I.

'You may laugh at me, if you like,' he said, 'but I believe it's an elemental. That's what I meant when I said it was a being half-way between the material and the ghostly. I never caught a glimpse of it till this afternoon; I only felt there was something horrible there. But now I've seen it, and it's like what spiritualists and that sort of folk describe as an elemental. A huge phosphorescent slug is what they tell us of it, which at will can surround itself with darkness.'

Somehow, now safe within doors, in the cheerful light and warmth of the room, the suggestion appeared merely grotesque. Out there in the darkness of that uncomfortable wood something within me had quaked, and I was prepared to believe any horror, but now common sense revolted.

'But you don't mean to tell me you believe in such rubbish?' I said. 'You might as well say it was a unicorn. What *is* an elemental, anyway? Who has ever seen one except the people who listen to raps in the darkness and say they are made by their aunts?'

'What is it, then?' he asked.

'I should think it is chiefly our own nerves,' I said. 'I frankly acknowledge I got the creeps when I went through the wood first, and I got them much worse when I went through it with you. But it was just nerves; we are frightening ourselves and each other.'

'And are the dogs frightening themselves and each other?' he asked. 'And the birds?'

That was rather harder to answer; in fact, I gave it up. Hugh continued.

'Well, just for the moment we'll suppose that something else, not ourselves, frightened us and the dogs and the birds,' he said, 'and that we did see something like a huge phosphorescent slug. I won't call it an elemental, if you object to that; I'll call it It. There's another thing, too, which the existence of It would explain.'

'What's that?' I asked.

'Well, It is supposed to be some incarnation of evil; it is a corporeal form of the devil. It is not only spiritual, it is material to this extent – that it can be seen, bodily in form, and heard, and, as you noticed, smelt, and, God forbid, handled. It has to be kept alive by nourishment. And that explains perhaps why, every day since I have been here, I've found on that knoll we went up some half-dozen dead rabbits.'

'Stoats and weasels,' said I.

'No, not stoats and weasels. Stoats kill their prey and eat it. These rabbits have not been eaten; they've been drunk.'

'What on earth do you mean?' I asked.

'I examined several of them. There was just a small hole in their throats, and they were drained of blood. Just skin and bones, and a sort of grey mash of fibre, like – like the fibre of an orange which has been sucked. Also there was a horrible smell lingering on them. And was the thing you had a glimpse of like a stoat or a weasel?'

There came a rattle at the handle of the door.

'Not a word to Daisy,' said Hugh as she entered.

'I heard you come in,' she said. 'Where did you go?'

'All round the place,' said I, 'and came back through the wood. It is odd; not a bird did we see; but that is partly accounted for because it was dark.'

I saw her eyes search Hugh's, but she found no communication there. I guessed that he was planning some attack on It next day, and he did not wish her to know that anything was afoot.

'The wood's unpopular,' he said. 'Birds won't go there, dogs won't go there, and Daisy won't go there. I'm bound to say I share the feeling too, but having braved its terrors in the dark I've broken the spell.'

'All quiet, was it?' asked she.

'Quiet wasn't the word for it. The smallest pin could have been heard dropping half a mile off.'

We talked over our plans that night after she had gone up to bed. Hugh's story about the sucked rabbits was rather horrible, and though there was no certain connection between those empty rinds of animals and what we had seen, there seemed a certain reasonableness about it. But anything, as he pointed out, which could feed like that was clearly not without its material side – ghosts did not have dinner, and if it was material it was vulnerable.

Our plans, therefore, were very simple; we were going to tramp through the wood, as one walks up partridges in a field of turnips, each with a shotgun and a supply of cartridges. I cannot say that I looked forward to the expedition, for I hated the thought of getting into closer quarters with that mysterious denizen of the woods; but there was a certain excitement about it, sufficient to keep me awake a long time, and when I got to sleep to cause very vivid and awful dreams.

The morning failed to fulfil the promise of the clear sunset; the sky was lowering and cloudy and a fine rain was falling. Daisy had shopping errands which took her into the little town, and as soon as she had set off we started on our business. The yellow retriever, mad with joy at the sight of guns, came bounding with us across the garden, but on our entering the wood he slunk back home again.

The wood was roughly circular in shape, with a diameter perhaps of half a mile. In the centre, as I have said, there was an open clearing about a quarter of a mile across, which was thus surrounded by a belt of thick trees and copse a couple of hundred yards in breadth. Our plan was first to walk together up the path which led through the wood, with all possible stealth, hoping to hear some movement on the part of what we had come to seek. Failing that, we had settled to tramp through the wood at the distance of some fifty yards from each other in a circular track; two or three of these circuits would cover the whole ground pretty thoroughly. Of the nature of our quarry, whether it would try to steal away from us, or possibly attack, we had no idea; it seemed, however, yesterday to have avoided us.

Rain had been falling steadily for an hour when we entered the wood; it hissed a little in the tree-tops overhead; but so thick was the cover that the ground below was still not more than damp. It was a dark morning outside; here you would say that the sun had already set and that night was falling. Very quietly we moved up the grassy path, where our footfalls were noiseless, and once we caught a whiff of that odour of live corruption; but though we stayed and listened not a sound of anything stirred except the sibilant rain over our heads. We went across the clearing and through to the far gate, and still there was no sign.

'We'll be getting into the trees, then,' said Hugh. 'We had better start where we got that whiff of it.'

We went back to the place, which was towards the middle of the encompassing trees. The odour still lingered on the windless air.

'Go on about fifty yards,' he said, 'and then we'll go in. If either of us comes on the track of it we'll shout to each other.'

I walked on down the path till I had gone the right distance, signalled to him, and we stepped in among the trees.

I have never known the sensation of such utter loneliness. I knew that Hugh was walking parallel with me, only fifty yards away, and if I hung on my step I could faintly hear his tread among the beech-leaves. But I felt as if I was quite sundered in this dim place from all companionship of man; the only live thing that lurked here was that monstrous mysterious creature of evil. So thick were the trees that I could not see more than a dozen yards in any direction; all places outside the wood seemed infinitely remote, and infinitely remote also everything that had occurred to me in normal human life. I had been whisked out of all wholesome experiences into this antique and evil place. The rain had ceased, it whispered no longer in the tree-tops, testifying that there did exist a world and a sky outside, and only a few drops from above pattered on the beech-leaves.

Suddenly I heard the report of Hugh's gun, followed by his shouting voice.

'I've missed it,' he shouted; 'it's coming in your direction.'

I heard him running towards me, the beech-leaves rustling, and no doubt his footsteps drowned a stealthier noise that was close to me. All that happened now, until once more I heard the report of Hugh's gun, happened, I suppose, in less than a minute. If it had taken much longer I do not imagine I should be telling it today.

I stood there then, having heard Hugh's shout, with my gun cocked, and ready to put to my shoulder, and I listened to his running footsteps. But still I saw nothing to shoot at and heard nothing. Then between two beech trees, quite close to me, I saw what I can only describe as a ball of darkness. It rolled very swiftly towards me over the few yards that separated me from it, and then, too late, I heard the dead beech-leaves rustling below it. Just before it reached me, my brain realised what it was, or what it might be, but before I could raise my gun to shoot at that nothingness it was upon me. My gun was twitched out of my hand, and I was enveloped in this blackness, which was the very essence of corruption. It knocked me off my feet, and I sprawled flat on my back, and upon me, as I lay there, I felt the weight of this invisible assailant.

I groped wildly with my hands and they clutched something cold and slimy and hairy. They slipped off it, and next moment there was laid across my shoulder and neck something which felt like an india-rubber tube. The end of it fastened on to my neck like a snake, and I felt the skin rise beneath it. Again, with clutching hands, I tried to tear that obscene strength away from me, and as I struggled with it I heard Hugh's footsteps close to me through this layer of darkness that hid everything.

My mouth was free, and I shouted at him.

'Here, here!' I yelled. 'Close to you, where it is darkest.'

I felt his hands on mine, and that added strength detached from my neck that sucker that pulled at it. The coil that lay heavy on my legs and chest writhed and struggled and relaxed. Whatever it was that our four hands held, slipped out of them, and I saw Hugh standing close to me. A yard or two off, vanishing among the beech trunks, was that blackness which had poured over me. Hugh put up his gun, and with his second barrel fired at it.

The blackness dispersed, and there, wriggling and twisting like a huge worm, lay what we had come to find. It was alive still, and I picked up my gun which lay by my side and fired two more barrels into it. The writhings dwindled into mere shudderings and shakings, and then it lay still.

With Hugh's help I got to my feet, and we both reloaded before going nearer. On the ground there lay a monstrous thing, half slug, half worm. There was no head to it; it ended in a blunt point with an orifice. In colour it was grey, covered with sparse black hairs; its length, I suppose, was some four feet, its thickness at the broadest part was that of a man's thigh, tapering towards each end. It was shattered by shot at its middle. There were stray pellets which had hit it elsewhere, and from the holes they had made there oozed not blood, but some grey viscous matter.

As we stood there some swift process of disintegration and decay began. It lost outline, it melted, it liquefied, and in a minute more we were looking at a mass of stained and coagulated beech-leaves. Again and quickly that liquor of corruption faded, and there lay at our feet no trace of what had been there. The overpowering odour passed away, and there came from the ground just the sweet savour of wet earth in springtime, and from above the glint of a sunbeam piercing the clouds. Then a sudden pattering among the dead leaves sent my heart into my mouth again, and I cocked my gun. But it was only Hugh's yellow retriever who had joined us.

We looked at each other.

'You're not hurt?' he said.

I held my chin up.

'Not a bit,' I said. 'The skin's not broken, is it?'

'No; only a round red mark. My God, what was it? What happened?'

'Your turn first,' said I. 'Begin at the beginning.'

'I came upon it quite suddenly,' he said. 'It was lying coiled like a sleeping dog behind a big beech. Before I could fire, it slithered off in the direction where I knew you were. I got a snapshot at it among the trees, but I must have missed, for I heard it rustling away. I shouted to you and ran after it. There was a circle of absolute darkness on the ground, and your voice came from the middle of it. I couldn't see you at all, but I clutched at the blackness and my hands met yours. They met something else too.'

We got back to the house and had put the guns away before Daisy came home from her shopping. We had also scrubbed and brushed and washed. She came into the smoking-room.

'You lazy folk,' she said. 'It has cleared up, and why are you still indoors? Let's go out at once.'

I got up.

'Hugh has told me you've got a dislike of the wood,' I said, 'and it's a lovely wood. Come and see; he and I will walk on each side of you and hold your hands. The dogs shall protect you as well.'

'But not one of them will go a yard into the wood,' said she.

'Oh yes, they will. At least, we'll try them. You must promise to come if they do.'

Hugh whistled them up, and down we went to the gate. They sat panting for it to be opened, and scuttled into the thickets in pursuit of interesting smells.

'And who says there are no birds in it?' said Daisy. 'Look at that robin! Why, there are two of them. Evidently house-hunting.'

Caterpillars

I saw a month or two ago in an Italian paper that the Villa Cascana, in which I once stayed, had been pulled down, and that a manufactory of some sort was in process of erection on its site. There is therefore no longer any reason for refraining from writing of those things which I myself saw (or imagined I saw) in a certain room and on a certain landing of the villa in question, nor from mentioning the circumstances which followed, which may or may not (according to the opinion of the reader) throw some light on or be somehow connected with this experience.

The Villa Cascana was in all ways but one a perfectly delightful house, yet, if it were standing now, nothing in the world – I use the phrase in its literal sense – would induce me to set foot in it again, for I believe it to have been haunted in a very terrible and practical manner. Most ghosts, when all is said and done, do not do much harm; they may perhaps terrify, but the person whom they visit usually gets over their visitation. They may on the other hand be entirely friendly and beneficent. But the appearances in the Villa Cascana were not beneficent, and had they made their 'visit' in a very slightly different manner, I do not suppose I should have got over it any more than Arthur Inglis did.

The house stood on an ilex-clad hill not far from Sestri di Levante on the Italian Riviera, looking out over the iridescent blues of that enchanted sea, while behind it rose the pale green chestnut woods that climb up the hill-sides till they give place to the pines that, black in contrast with them, crown the slopes. All round it the garden in the luxuriance of mid-spring bloomed and was fragrant, and the scent of magnolia and rose, borne on the salt freshness of the winds from the sea, flowed like a stream through the cool vaulted rooms.

On the ground floor a broad pillared *loggia* ran round three sides of the house, the top of which formed a balcony for certain rooms of the first floor. The main staircase, broad and of grey marble steps, led up from the hall to the landing outside these rooms, which were three in number, namely, two big sitting-rooms and a bedroom arranged *en suite*. The latter was unoccupied, the sitting-rooms were in use. From these the main staircase was continued to the second floor, where were situated certain bedrooms, one of which I occupied, while from the other side of the first-floor landing some half-dozen steps led to another suite of rooms, where, at the time I am speaking of, Arthur Inglis, the artist, had his bedroom and studio. Thus the landing outside my bedroom at the top of the house commanded both the landing of the first floor and also the steps that led to Inglis's rooms. Jim Stanley and his wife, finally (whose guest I was), occupied rooms in another wing of the house, where also were the servants' quarters.

I arrived just in time for lunch on a brilliant noon of mid-May. The garden was shouting with colour and fragrance, and not less delightful after my broiling walk up from the *marina*, should have been the coming from the reverberating heat and blaze of the day into the marble coolness of the villa. Only (the reader has my bare word for this, and nothing more), the moment I set foot in the house I felt that something was wrong. This feeling, I may say, was quite vague, though very strong, and I remember that when I saw letters waiting for me on the table in the hall I felt certain that the explanation was here: I was convinced that there was bad news of some sort for me. Yet when I opened them I found no such explanation of my premonition: my correspondents all reeked of prosperity. Yet this clear miscarriage of a presentiment did not dissipate my uneasiness. In that cool fragrant house there was something wrong.

I am at pains to mention this because to the general view it may explain that though I am as a rule so excellent a sleeper that the extinction of my light on getting into bed is apparently contemporaneous with being called on the following morning, I slept very badly on my first night in the Villa Cascana. It may also explain the fact that when I did sleep (if it was indeed in sleep that I saw what I thought I saw) I dreamed in a very vivid and original manner, original, that is to say, in the sense that something that, as far as I knew, had never previously entered into my consciousness, usurped it then. But since, in addition to this evil premonition, certain words and events occurring during the rest of the day might have suggested something of what I thought happened that night, it will be well to relate them.

After lunch, then, I went round the house with Mrs Stanley, and during our tour she referred, it is true, to the unoccupied bedroom on the first floor, which opened out of the room where we had lunched.

'We left that unoccupied,' she said, 'because Jim and I have a charming bedroom and dressing-room, as you saw, in the wing, and if we used it ourselves we should have to turn the dining-room into a dressing-room and have our meals downstairs. As it is, however, we have our little flat there, Arthur Inglis has his little flat in the other passage; and I remembered (aren't I extraordinary?) that you once said that the higher up you were in a house the better you were pleased. So I put you at the top of the house, instead of giving you that room.'

It is true, that a doubt, vague as my uneasy premonition, crossed my mind at this. I did not see why Mrs Stanley should have explained all this, if there had not been more to explain. I allow, therefore, that the thought that there was something to explain about the unoccupied bedroom was momentarily present to my mind.

The second thing that may have borne on my dream was this.

At dinner the conversation turned for a moment on ghosts. Inglis, with the certainty of conviction, expressed his belief that anybody who could possibly believe in the existence of supernatural phenomena was unworthy of the name of an ass. The subject instantly dropped. As far as I can recollect, nothing else occurred or was said that could bear on what follows.

We all went to bed rather early, and personally I yawned my way upstairs, feeling hideously sleepy. My room was rather hot, and I threw all the windows wide, and from without poured in the white light of the moon, and the love-song of many nightingales. I undressed quickly, and got into bed, but though I had felt so sleepy before, I now felt extremely wide-awake. But I was quite content to be awake: I did not toss or turn, I felt perfectly happy listening to the song and seeing the light. Then, it is possible, I may have gone to sleep, and what follows may have been a dream. I thought, anyhow, that after a time the nightingales ceased singing and the moon sank. I thought also that if, for some unexplained reason, I was going to lie awake all night, I might as well read, and I remembered that I had left a book in which I was interested in the dining-room on the first floor. So I got out of bed, lit a candle, and went downstairs. I went into the room, saw on a side-table the book I had come to look for, and then, simultaneously, saw that the door into the unoccupied bedroom was open. A curious grey light, not of dawn nor of moonshine, came out of it, and I looked in. The bed stood just opposite the door, a big four-poster, hung with tapestry at the head. Then I saw that the greyish light of the bedroom came from the bed, or rather from what was on the bed. For it was covered with great caterpillars, a foot or more in length, which crawled over it. They were faintly luminous, and it was the light from them that showed me the room. Instead of the sucker-feet of ordinary caterpillars they had rows of pincers like crabs, and they moved by grasping what they lay on with their pincers, and then sliding their bodies forward. In colour these dreadful insects were yellowish-grey, and they were covered with irregular lumps and swellings. There must have been hundreds of them, for they formed a sort of writhing, crawling pyramid on the bed. Occasionally one fell off on to the floor, with a soft fleshy thud, and though the floor was of hard concrete, it yielded to the pincer feet as if it had been putty, and, crawling back, the caterpillar would mount on to the bed again, to rejoin its fearful companions. They appeared to have no faces, so to speak, but at one end of them there was a mouth that opened sideways in respiration.

Then, as I looked, it seemed to me as if they all suddenly became conscious of my presence. All the mouths, at any rate, were turned in my direction, and next moment they began dropping off the bed with those soft fleshy thuds on to the floor, and wriggling towards me. For one second a paralysis as of a dream was on me, but the next I was running upstairs again to my room, and I remember feeling the cold of the marble steps on my bare feet. I rushed into my bedroom, and slammed the door behind me, and then – I was certainly wide-awake now – I found myself standing by my bed with the sweat of terror pouring from me. The noise of the banged door still rang in my ears. But, as would have been more usual, if this had been mere nightmare, the terror that had been mine when I saw those foul beasts crawling about the bed or dropping softly on to the floor did not cease then. Awake now, if dreaming before, I did not at all recover from the horror of dream: it did not seem to me that I had dreamed. And until dawn, I sat or stood, not daring to lie down, thinking that every rustle or movement that I heard was the approach of the caterpillars. To them and the claws that bit into the cement the wood of the door was child's play: steel would not keep them out.

But with the sweet and noble return of day the horror vanished: the whisper of wind became benignant again: the nameless fear, whatever it was, was smoothed out and terrified me no longer. Dawn broke, hueless at first; then it grew dove-coloured, then the flaming pageant of light spread over the sky.

*

The admirable rule of the house was that everybody had breakfast where and when he pleased, and in consequence it was not till lunch-time that I met any of the other members of our party, since I had breakfast on my balcony, and wrote letters and other things till lunch. In fact, I got down to that meal rather late, after the other three had begun. Between my knife and fork there was a small pill-box of cardboard, and as I sat down Inglis spoke.

'Do look at that,' he said, 'since you are interested in natural history. I found it crawling on my counterpane last night, and I don't know what it is.'

I think that before I opened the pill-box I expected something of the sort which I found in it. Inside it, anyhow, was a small caterpillar, greyish-yellow in colour, with curious bumps and excrescences on its rings. It was extremely active, and hurried round the box, this way and that. Its feet were unlike the feet of any caterpillar I ever saw: they were like the pincers of a crab. I looked, and shut the lid down again.

'No, I don't know it,' I said, 'but it looks rather unwholesome. What are you going to do with it?'

'Oh, I shall keep it,' said Inglis. 'It has begun to spin: I want to see what sort of a moth it turns into.'

I opened the box again, and saw that these hurrying movements were indeed the beginning of the spinning of the web of its cocoon. Then Inglis spoke again.

'It has got funny feet, too,' he said. 'They are like crabs' pincers. What's the Latin for crab? Oh, yes, Cancer. So in case it is unique, let's christen it: "Cancer Inglisensis".'

Then something happened in my brain, some momentary piecing together of all that I had seen or dreamed. Something in his words seemed to me to throw light on it all, and my own intense horror at the experience of the night before linked itself on to what he had just said. In effect, I took the box and threw it, caterpillar and all, out of the window. There was a gravel path just outside, and beyond it, a fountain playing into a basin. The box fell on to the middle of this.

Inglis laughed.

'So the students of the occult don't like solid facts,' he said. 'My poor caterpillar!'

The talk went off again at once on to other subjects, and I have only given in detail, as they happened, these trivialities in order to be sure myself that I have recorded everything that could have borne on occult subjects or on the subject of caterpillars. But at the moment when I threw the pill-box into the fountain, I lost my head: my only excuse is that, as is probably plain, the tenant of it was, in miniature, exactly what I had seen crowded on to the bed in the unoccupied room. And though this translation of those phantoms into flesh and blood – or whatever it is that caterpillars are made of – ought perhaps to have relieved the horror of the night, as a matter of fact it did nothing of the kind. It only made the crawling pyramid that covered the bed in the unoccupied room more hideously real.

After lunch we spent a lazy hour or two strolling about the garden or sitting in the *loggia*, and it must have been about four o'clock when Stanley and I started off to bathe, down the path that led by the fountain into which I had thrown the pill-box. The water was shallow and clear, and at the bottom of it I saw its white remains. The water had disintegrated the cardboard, and it had become no more than a few strips and shreds of sodden paper. The centre of the fountain was a marble Italian Cupid which squirted the water out of a wine-skin held under its arm. And crawling up its leg was the caterpillar. Strange and scarcely credible as it seemed, it must have survived the falling-to-bits of its prison, and made its way to shore, and there it was, out of arm's reach, weaving and waving this way and that as it evolved its cocoon.

Then, as I looked at it, it seemed to me again that, like the caterpillar I had seen last night, it saw me, and breaking out of the threads that surrounded it, it crawled down the marble leg of the Cupid and began swimming like a snake across the water of the fountain towards me. It came with extraordinary speed (the fact of a caterpillar being able to swim was new to me), and in another moment was crawling up the marble lip of the basin. Just then Inglis joined us.

'Why, if it isn't old "Cancer Inglisensis" again,' he said, catching sight of the beast. 'What a tearing hurry it is in!'

We were standing side by side on the path, and when the caterpillar had advanced to within about a yard of us, it stopped, and began waving again as if in doubt as to the direction in which it should go. Then it appeared to make up its mind, and crawled on to Inglis's shoe.

'It likes me best,' he said, 'but I don't really know that I like it. And as it won't drown I think perhaps –'

He shook it off his shoe on to the gravel path and trod on it.

All afternoon the air got heavier and heavier with the Sirocco that was without doubt coming up from the south, and that night again I went up to bed feeling very sleepy; but below my drowsiness, so to speak, there was the consciousness, stronger than before, that there was something wrong in the house, that something dangerous was close at hand. But I fell asleep at once, and – how long after I do not know – either woke or dreamed I awoke, feeling that I must get up at once, *or I should be too late*. Then (dreaming or awake) I lay and fought this fear, telling myself that I was but the prey of my own nerves disordered by Sirocco or what not, and at the same time quite clearly knowing in another part of my mind, so to speak, that every moment's delay added to the danger. At last this second feeling became irresistible, and I put on coat and trousers and went out of my room on to the landing. And then I saw that I had already delayed too long, and that I was now too late.

The whole of the landing of the first floor below was invisible under the swarm of caterpillars that crawled there. The folding doors into the sitting-room from which opened the bedroom where I had seen them last night were shut, but they were squeezing through the cracks of it and dropping one by one through the keyhole, elongating themselves into mere string as they passed, and growing fat and lumpy again on emerging. Some, as if exploring, were nosing about the steps into the passage at the end of which were Inglis's rooms, others were crawling on the lowest steps of the staircase that led up to where I stood. The landing, however, was completely covered with them: I was cut off. And of the frozen horror that seized me when I saw that I can give no idea in words.

Then at last a general movement began to take place, and they grew thicker on the steps that led to Inglis's room. Gradually, like some hideous tide of flesh, they advanced along the passage, and I saw the foremost, visible by the pale grey luminousness that came from them, reach his door. Again and again I tried to shout and warn him, in terror all the time that they would turn at the sound of my voice and mount my stair instead, but for all my efforts I felt that no sound came from my throat. They crawled along the hinge-crack of his door, passing through as they had done before, and still I stood there, making impotent efforts to shout to him, to bid him escape while there was time.

At last the passage was completely empty: they had all gone, and at that moment I was conscious for the first time of the cold of the marble landing on which I stood barefooted. The dawn was just beginning to break in the Eastern sky.

Six months after I met Mrs Stanley in a country house in England. We talked on many subjects and at last she said: 'I don't think I have seen you since I got that dreadful news about Arthur Inglis a month ago.'

'I haven't heard,' said I.

'No? He has got cancer. They don't even advise an operation, for there is no hope of a cure: he is riddled with it, the doctors say.'

Now during all these six months I do not think a day had passed on which I had not had in my mind the dreams (or whatever you like to call them) which I had seen in the Villa Cascana.

'It is awful, is it not?' she continued, 'and I feel I can't help feeling, that he may have – '

'Caught it at the villa?' I asked.

She looked at me in blank surprise.

'Why did you say that?' she asked. 'How did you know?'

Then she told me. In the unoccupied bedroom a year before there had been a fatal case of cancer. She had, of course, taken the best advice and had been told that the utmost dictates of prudence would be obeyed so long as she did not put anybody to sleep in the room, which had also been thoroughly disinfected and newly white-washed and painted. But –